BILLY JONES'S FATHER

And the Apple Tree

Fred Engh

Published by AMZProhub
Cover Designer: Fred Carson

CONTRIBUTING EDITOR

JOANNA WILKINSON

DEDICATION

Some of us are lucky to have had someone who made a life-changing experience for us. For me, it was a guy named Paul Fink. It would take too long to describe how one move by Paul changed the life of my family and me forever.

I'm sure Paul isn't around anymore, but somehow I still want to thank him. Maybe this will do.

1

"Oh, my Lord, Dad!" Sara cried out in her Texas drawl as the sign saying, *Welcome to North Carolina* appeared. "This sure isn't Texas."

Breathing in the fresh smell of thousands of azaleas and rhododendrons with their spicy, clove odor lining the highway, she couldn't contain herself, "I think I'm already beginning to like North Carolina."

In the distance, mountain after mountain, looking like an ocean filled with hurricane-size waves, welcomed the Tobins to their new home.

"We're in Carolina!" an overexcited Jeff sang out. "Get that James Taylor CD, Sara. I want to hear *Carolina in My Mind*."

As soon as the song came on, the family of three began to join along, sounding like a bunch of teenagers on their way to the beach while drowning out poor James Taylor with their exuberance.

"Those are the Blue Ridge mountains, aren't they, Dad?" asked Sara. Other than when she went off to college, Sara had never been too far from home.

"They sure are, kid," Jeff said as his wife Amanda sat full of thought about what lay ahead. She was excited about her new life and wondered what kind of impact she could have on a small town like Torrid Hills as a child psychologist.

No sooner had they rounded a hill that had blocked the late afternoon sun shining in their eyes, a sign popped up saying, "Exit 24 to Torrid Hills". While taking the exit, a sky-high drone-like vision of small-town America lay in the distant valley below. A water tank with big black letters saying, *Welcome to Torrid Hills*, urged Sara to say, so loud that the folks in town could probably hear her, "WE MADE IT!" They had reached their new hometown, and welcoming them were gigantic red maple trees, waving like blankets in the breeze.

Torrid Hills was a typical small town in North Carolina with a population of 24,000, most of whom worked in the tobacco industry. Jeff had been hired by the national medical firm First Med as their local representative physician for the town.

"Sara, look for twenty-six Brentwood Street on your cell phone. That's the address of our new home." Jeff said.

An excited Amanda eyed the colonial-style homes when Sara yelled out, "There it is, Dad!"

Sure enough, right in the middle of Brentwood Street stood a two-story home covered with ivy. It didn't take long before the three unpacked their initial belongings and began to settle into their new home.

On their first Monday in town, Jeff left early to visit his new office at *First Med*. Amanda, anxious to begin her journey as the town's only child psychologist, scoured the "*office space*" ads in the Torrid Hills Times. As for Sara, she sought to seek out the local recreation department for any employment available. It didn't take long. She could see the sign above the recreation facility a mere block from her house saying *Torrid Hills Parks and Recreation*. Sara wasn't one to waste time. She dressed and was almost out the door when Amanda said, "Wow, you're not even going to eat breakfast before you go?"

"No time for that, Mom," Sara answered. "A stitch in time saves nine."

Walking in the recreation front door, Sara was met with a voice sounding more like Scarlett O'Hara than Scarlett herself. "Good morning, ma'am." said the voice reminding Sara that she was in the South.

6

"Good morning to you," Sara replied. "I just moved in from out of town. Texas, to be exact. I was wondering if there might be any employment openings?"

Just then, around the corner, came a lady who looked to be in her mid-thirties, dressed like she was about to enter a hog-tying event.

"Hey there. I'm Emma Stewart. I couldn't help but overhear that you're looking for employment. You've come at the right time if you have the right credentials."

"I do," Sara said as she grabbed a resume from her backpack.

"Well, great," Emma said as she glanced at Sara's resume. "Why don't you come to my office and have a little chat about what's available."

Feeling enthused, Sara sat down in Emma's office and glanced at the number of trophies strewn about.

"Wow, there must be a big event going on with all these trophies," Sara said.

"You're looking at a small number of trophies that we will be giving out this year. Trophies for every sport you can imagine. We give them to kids in the three- to the five-year-old division up to the sixteen- to eighteen-year-olds. This town is crazy about sports."

"Well, it sounds like I came to the right town. My background is in sports," Sara said.

Looking through Sara's resume, Emma's eyebrows raised as she noticed the number of awards Sara had gained playing all sports.

"You certainly are qualified, especially with the degree you got in recreation," Emma said. "I need an assistant to cover a lot of details that are getting overwhelming for me. That is if you're interested."

"Absolutely," Sara replied while almost coming out of her seat. "I'm ready to start whenever you want."

"Well, it's Friday. How about we start on Monday," Emma noted with a smile.

"Great!" Sara answered as if she had just won the state lottery.

2

"I'll tell you one thing. My dad kicked ass," Arnold proclaimed in his usual braggadocio manner to the five regulars who met most afternoons at *Andy's Bar and Grill*. All five worked at the Torrid Hills Tobacco Industry (THTI), owned by Scotty Jones, Arnold's dad. It only took a couple of beers before it became customary to listen to Arnold pontificate on the athletic heroics of his father. But the group had little choice but to appease Arnold as he rambled on about one episode after another. He was, after all, the general manager of his dad, Scotty's, THTI business.

It was strange hearing Arnold talk about his father's athletic skills. After all, Arnold himself was a failure at every sport he tried. And the group knew it. When Arnold wasn't looking, Al Simpson would roll his eyes in mockery as Arnold continued. The others had the faces of Sunday parishioners listening to the good reverend asking for more money from the congregation. Arnold's dad had tried desperately to make Arnold another athlete to shine in the Jones family athletic tree. But, poor Arnold seemingly tripped over his two left feet like a drunken sailor walking the ship's deck in the middle of a tropical storm. But Arnold wouldn't give up.

"Why don't you try music like your sister, Arnold?" his grandfather would plead. "My dad was the greatest, and I will be just as famous. Just watch." Arnold would announce at ten years old.

When he played baseball, he would overrun an outfield fly ball so badly that the other team's player on second base would have no trouble making it to home plate. Most of his coaches wouldn't think of cutting Arnold from the team. By cutting him, they knew they would suffer Scotty's irrational reaction. They yearned for Arnold to have some of his father's talent. But it wasn't meant to be.

Not all coaches bowed like scared sheep to Scotty's pressure. Arnold's little league baseball coach, Lionel Massey, had had enough of Scotty's overbearing influence. It all came crashing down during Arnold's first year in little league.

"What's the matter with you, Lionel?' Scotty would yell as he fidgeted in his seat, watching them practice. "Whoever let you coach this team? Put my boy in Lionel!" he would scream, "Or you won't be coaching this team again. I know the head of this league, and he'll have your ass out of here in a heartbeat."

Arnold would lift his shoulders as if trying to hide his head under his shirt in embarrassment. The other players stared at him like he was a wounded puppy wanting to hide under a fence.

Lionel dropped him from the team when Arnold struck out four times in the season's first game. Arnold cried as he walked the five blocks to his home. Being cut by Coach Lionel was the least of his problems. He knew telling his father would mean a certain beating. But he was in for a surprise. Walking in the door, trembling with fear, he said, "Dad, Coach Lionel cut me from the team."

Scotty had a ferocious temper, brought on by bipolar disorder, some suggested, the result of serving in Vietnam. It took very little to set him off. The crying words out of Arnold's mouth did just that. Like a stone thrown into a wasp nest, Scotty stormed out of the house, into his car, and rushed to the ballfield, knocking over almost every trash can lining the streets.

Slamming on the brakes, he jumped from the car and headed towards the field. Lionel stood with mouth gaping as he trembled at the sight of what looked to be a ferocious leopard about to attack him.

"You fucking bastard! That's my son, you cut." With that, he hauled off and landed his right fist on Lionel's jaw, sending him floating to the ground like a sheet falling off a clothesline in a windstorm.

The townsfolk ignored Lionel's plea to have Scotty arrested. He was Scotty Jones, and no one wanted to intervene. Back home, running his hands through his hair and pacing back and forth across the floor, a disgruntled Scotty suddenly blurted out to his wife Martha, "Why don't we enroll him in one of those sports camps? They ought to bring out his talent somewhere in that body."

"Great idea," Martha said in delight.

They tried, but after two weeks, Harry Whitfield, the camp director, threw his hands up in frustration. Arnold did not have what it took to be any kind of athlete. He told the Jones' that they were wasting their money trying to make a silk purse from a sow's ear.

In his mind, Arnold became a failure to the parents he so wanted to please. He sat, depressed in his room night after night. His failed little league days were over.

When Arnold was about fourteen years old, like a tsunami wave about to wreak havoc, the old torment was to reappear. Scotty announced, "Arnold, your mom, and I have been talking about your going to high school and how you might be one of those what psychologists call 'late matures.' We figure that might be why you never did well playing little league. You think that might be why you stunk out there on the field?"

"Gosh, I don't know, Dad, but are you saying you want me to go out for high school sports?"

"What the hell do you think I was talking about?" Scotty yelled back. "Of course, if you want to sign up for a sewing class, we could arrange for you to do that," he said with a glare. Arnold pinched his lips tightly to keep them from trembling.

A few months later, when it came time for Arnold to go to high school, he had no choice but to sign up for sports. To avoid the wrath of Scotty, he signed up every season for a sports team. And, of course, the coaches in high school also feared the rage of Scotty if they didn't include Arnold on the team. His fellow players knew what was happening and, behind the coach's back, became unmerciful to Arnold. Once, they hid all his clothes in the locker room trash can. Another time they filled his locker with shaving cream. But worst of all was the verbal hazing he faced as a "loser" whenever he set foot on the court or field.

It all began during basketball season. At one game, Coach Tommy Alexander, feeling Scotty's glare like a six-inch knife entering his back, put Arnold in during the last few minutes. Arnold cost the team the game. In the last ten seconds, he, by mistake, threw the ball to an opposing team player who rushed down the court to score the winning shot. Scotty came running to the court. Screaming at the top of his voice, "YOU BUM, YOU CAN NEVER DO ANYTHING RIGHT." *1

Scotty and Martha never gave up hope. Well, at least Scotty didn't. He often attended Arnold's games, thinking that a day would come when he would do something that wasn't a complete disaster.

This day wasn't that day. Arnold dropped an easy pass in the end zone of the football game that would have given his team the win. Arnold was devastated and feared the tongue-lashing he would get as he rode home in the backseat. As Scotty and Martha sat up front, Arnold's mother, a red-faced, fiery woman, blasted Arnold as never before. He sat feeling dejected and rejected. "Do you realize how much you embarrassed us out there?" Arnold's mother yelled demeaning and hateful words. "I've seen a lot of football games where I was proudly watching your father play, but never have I seen anyone as awful as you out there looking like a fool. How do you think it makes us look in front of all those people? Your daddy was a hero around here, and now you go about destroying his legacy. You are a complete failure in our eyes!" she yelled with a voice screaming with hate and anger. *2

Thus, was the young life of Arnold Jones.

*1 This happened at a junior ice hockey game in Minneapolis.

*2 A district judge in Alabama told this story at a national meeting of recreation directors about his own experience.

3

Monday arrived. Sara couldn't wait to start her new job. Fiddling around her bedroom with an empty pit in her stomach, she picked up a pair of jeans and then, being on edge, threw them to the side.

"What should I wear, Mom? Should I dress casually or professionally? I can't decide," she cried out as if she were Cinderella going to the Ball. "I'm so nervous I can't see straight."

"Wear your nice, pleated skirt and that white blouse I got you for Christmas," Amanda answered in a motherly tone.

"Okay, I hope you're right. I don't want to look like some doofus on my first day." Sara said with a smirk on her face. She couldn't wait to get out the door and walk down the street to the recreation department office, where she knew Emma would be waiting.

"Good morning, Sara," Emma said, glancing at Sara's neat attire. "I guess they didn't tell you in college that recreation work doesn't require getting dressed up. But that's my bad. "

"Oh, I'm sorry," Sara replied as her eyes sheepishly looked at her new white blouse and pleated skirt. *And under her breath, saying, 'Why do I listen to my mother.'* "I wanted you to know that a girl from Texas wore more than cowboy boots and jeans."

"Not a problem. Let's take a walk out to the new complex we built."

No sooner had they walked out of the door than Scotty Jones rode by shouting at the top of his lungs, "Hey Emma, Let's get that new sign put up. Not that I'm trying to brag or anything." he said.

"It will be going up sooner than you think, Mr. Jones," Emma yelled back with more than a hint of patronization.

"Who was that?" Sara wondered out loud.

"That was Torrid Hill's gift from God. Or he thinks as much." Emma declared. "You know how you Texans talk about everything in Texas being big? Scotty has such a big head that it wouldn't fit in the whole state of Texas."

"I take it he's not one of your favorite people here In Torrid Hills?" asked Sara.

"You'd be just about right." Emma acknowledged. "It won't take long before you know what I mean."

"Wow, this complex looks great!" Sara said as she perused the landscape full of fields for baseball, football, soccer, and an assortment of other recreational offerings.

"We're having the grand opening next Saturday, so you're just in time to be part of it." Emma spelled out. "And guess who will be the center of attention for the whole thing?"

"Don't tell me it's the guy that just rode by asking where the sign was?" Sara questioned Emma.

"Yep, we're going to have a sign hung right over there at the entrance." She pointed. "It will have *Scotty Jones Athletic Complex* on it in big, bold letters."

"S'cuse my French Emma, but who the hell *IS* Scotty Jones, and why does he get the field named after him?"

"Now, I shouldn't be talking out of school to someone new like yourself, but you might as well know now rather than later," Emma replied.

"I got to know Scotty when I moved here to take over the rec program. The first day I walked out to one of the baseball fields, I could hear him screaming and hollering from the stands at the refs. He was relentless. We've had several refs quit because of his badgering them over calls they made. Especially when his son was involved. I know more about Scotty than his obnoxious behavior on the ball fields. But I'm not about to share that with you or anyone else. My best advice is to stay as far away from him as possible."

"Why on earth is his name being put up on this complex?" Sara asked.

"It goes way back, Sara. He was a war hero to most and was the best athlete to come out of Torrid Hills before that. So, the good 'ol boys still remember and don't care about his personal life. Therefore, up goes the sign".

"Wow, they never had any classes about that kind of stuff in our college rec program," Sara told Emma with disbelief.

"Maybe they should have," Emma responded. "The thing that makes Torrid Hills so challenging for us in recreation is the history around here."

"How so?" Sara asked, glancing at Emma, wondering if she might be getting into something she should have thought more about before accepting the job.

"The people around here are obsessed with winning. So much so that we've had someone get killed at a youth football game." Emma answered back with a tinge of anger in her voice.

"You're kidding me," Sara gasped, not believing the words she had just heard. And then blasted out. "Killed!? What happened?"

"It was a regular Saturday morning scheduled football game between two eight to ten-year-old teams. You knew something was going to happen in this game because the last time the two teams had played, things got very tense. The referees warned the parents that they would stop the game if they caused any problems. Towards the end of the game, the referee called an offsides penalty against one of the teams, and all hell broke loose. Parents came running out of the stands to the field. The kids stood there looking terrified as if someone had let a bunch of lions out of their cages. Parents were screaming and hollering at the referee when suddenly, a loud boom went off. Someone had a gun and shot a coach on the opposite team. He lay bleeding on the ground. People scattered everywhere. Parents grabbed their kids, who were now crying hysterically. I mean, it was bedlam!" shouted Emma, whose blood pressure seemed to have exceeded its limit. *

"Eight to ten-year-old kids?! And someone is getting killed because they didn't like the referee's call? That's just awful!" Sara exclaimed.

"Like I said," Emma commented. "This town is crazy when it comes to sports, and the sad thing is that no one has done anything about it. So, it just goes on and on. You'll see."

"Okay, enough scaring you about the job Sara," Emma said, trying to sound more comforting than she felt inside. "Let's go back inside, and I'll give you the rest of the day to set up your office."

The late afternoon clouds were aligned to look as if a thin layer of watercolors had been brushed across the far-off mountains. Sara walked home with her mind wandering helter-skelter.

"How'd everything go today at your new job, Sara?" Dr. Jeff asked.

"Well, one, I think I'm going to like my new boss. And two, I got here at the perfect time. She needed a new assistant. After we talked for a while, she offered me the job. And three, I think I'm in for more than I thought before we got here.

How did it go for you guys?" Sara asked her mom and dad.

"They needed a doctor here in Torrid Hills more than I imagined. My first day was jammed with patients." Jeff stated, shaking his head in disbelief.

"I guess my day was quiet compared to you two," Amanda chuckled. "But it takes time for people to realize that there is now someone in town who can answer questions about their kids growing up."

"After my conversation with my new boss Emma, I think you might be in the right town, at the right time also, Mom," Sara said to Amanda with a sense of uneasiness.

This event happened at a youth football game in Dallas.

4

Emma Townsend grew up in the town of Cutrusville, Florida. I know It sounds like it should be Citrusville, but somehow it got named Cutrusville. Of course, if you listened to the people talk in Cutrusville, you'd understand. The people there have a Southerner sound that would make Northerners try their best to understand one word from another.

Riding into town on Route 54, you'd have thought you were in some fantasyland straight out of Disneyworld. Gigantic citrus trees hung like hammocks along the streets. You could almost grab one right out of the car window. Orange trees, grapefruit, lemon, lime, it didn't matter. To no one's surprise, it seemed that practically everyone in Cutrusville worked in the citrus industry, even Emma Townsend. That was, of course, when she wasn't enrolled in Cutrusville High School.

Emma's dad, Gary Townsend, was the superintendent of the Clockback Orange Plant. A likable guy, Gary and his wife Dolly had one child… Emma. Being the only child, she was spoiled rotten and got her way at every turn. One time she and her eight-year-old friends decided to create a prank along the highway coming into Cutrusville. When no cars were in sight, they would rush out onto the road and lay oranges one by one in a line across the road. Of course, when cars came by, they would run over the oranges, and juice would fly everywhere, especially on the driver's cars. It didn't take long before one fuming driver stopped when he saw the girls hiding behind a clump of grapefruit trees. He called the police on his cell phone, and within minutes they were at the scene. The girls panicked when police officer Bert Philips decided to take them to their homes and tell their parents what had happened. Two of the girls were scared to death, but not Emma. She knew her single dad would think it was funny. Emma's mother had passed away when Emma was seven, and her father was left to care for his rambunctious daughter. Emma kept her shenanigans up throughout her early years. She was the local "tomboy." And thankfully, in time, sports took the place of Emma's rowdiness.

As Emma grew into adolescence, her athletic skills equaled that of most of the boys in town. She'd challenge boys to races and beat most at every chance. When it came time for "little league" baseball, she demanded to play on the boys' teams, and though it was unheard of, no one wondered why. Emma was that good.

Turning eleven years old, Emma was chosen for the Cutrusville "little league" team called the Rockets. They qualified for the regional tournament, in Softspring, FL. No one from Cutrusville gave it a thought that their opponents in the tournament might have opposition to having a girl on the team. That is until they reached the town of Softspring, where eighteen teams from throughout north Florida gathered for the playoffs.

Emma stood out like a tomato in a box of oranges as she and the male players stepped out of the team van dressed in their team uniforms.

The eyes of players and coaches on the other teams lit up, looking like they were watching scenes from a horror movie, as Emma and her team sauntered around like confident soldiers ready for battle. The echoing sounds from the growing crowd, seeing the presence of a *girl,* sounded like a massive horde of bees searching for honey. "What's she doing here?" one coach walked around asking as if he were the lord almighty. "Ain't no girl gonna be playing on a team in this tournament!" probed another. Soon the murmurs spread so fast you would have thought someone had planted a hydrogen bomb in the vicinity. All along, Emma took it in stride, probably because of the "spoiled brat" in her. No one was going to intimidate her. And she was about to show them a girl can play just as well as boys, probably better.

The Rockets from Cutrusville crushed every team they faced while Emma led the way. Spectators were stunned that "a girl" could be *that* good. When the Rockets were presented with the winning trophy, Emma took the stage to receive it. All the parents and coaches on the other teams couldn't believe what they were seeing... a *girl* receiving the trophy. And then Emma let loose.

"Y'all a bunch of backwoods, redneck hillbillies for thinkin' a girl can't play as good as boys." She screamed so loud you might have heard her in the next town over. She stormed off the stage kissing the trophy in one hand and the middle finger up with the other. The crowd sat there with their mouths open as wide as the largest wide-mouth bass ever caught in North Florida.

Funny thing about Emma; by the time she went to high school, her tomboy looks turned into glamorous looks. Guys eyed her everywhere she turned. But she spurned them away. She had other thoughts. She remained the torchbearer for girls in sports. Throughout the years, while she played on the girls' basketball, volleyball, and softball teams, she had one more challenge.... football.

"No, no, no," her dad cried out as if he had seen his last bottle of beer about to fall onto their tile floor. "Football is a boy's game. You'll get hurt. Boys on other teams won't like it and will be gunning for you. I know you want to prove something, but football is not a sport you want to fool with."

Emma had a hard time arguing with her dad. She had seen several of her classmates being carried off the field. Some permanently injured.

"How about I try out for kicker?" she said with a confident smile on her face.

"You're kidding, right?" he replied as his mouth scrunched up. "You've never kicked a football in your life."

"But I can learn," Emma said emphatically. "How about if you build me a goal post out back, and I'll start practicing. I promise you I'll make the team. C'mon, Dad!"

"Your mother would have thought I was nuts to let you get away with all I have since she passed, but once again, you win, Miss Spoiled Brat."

A week later, there in the backyard stood a regulation field goal hidden away so no one would wonder why a goalpost was at Emma's house.

It was off-season when Emma snuck into the boy's locker room, where equipment was behind a wire cage. The metal door was unlocked, and inside were close to fifteen footballs in the corner. Grabbing four of them in her arms, she shoved them, one by one, under her father's Florida Gator's football shirt. She looked like the Pillsbury doughboy as she eased her way out to the car where her dad sat waiting.

"I must be a damn fool!" Gary lamented. "I could go to jail for helping my daughter steal footballs. How crazy is this?"

"But I'm going to return them, Dad," Emma said, sounding like an innocent kid with her fingers in the cookie jar.

"I'll tell you one thing, Missy. You better make this all worthwhile." Gary announced to his thankful daughter.

Emma vowed that all this effort would not be in vain. All summer long, through wind and rain, she would be out back practicing her kicking. 25 yards, 30 yards, and even 40 yards kicks.

When football practice began in late August, Emma showed up, but not before she snuck the worn-out footballs back into the cage.

"Hi, coach," Emma yelled to Coach Tom Carter as she ran out to the field filled with anticipation.

'Nice to see you, Emma. Looking forward to your last year in school?" Coach Carter said, never thinking as to what he was about to hear.

"Yep, and I'm here to try out for the team," Emma announced.

"You what?" the incredulous coach said with his lips curled up while biting his teeth.

'I know what you're thinking, coach." Emma announced, knowing the coach thought she was off her rocker. "I think I could be the best placekicker this team has ever seen."

"Look, I know all about your history with women being able to play every sport. But you, a kicker?" he said with a hint of disgust. "Have you ever kicked a football?"

"OK, I understand you don't want to waste time with me, but how about you give me a try?" Emma said while appearing to beg. "Here's the deal. Let's go to the field, and if I hit three out of three from thirty yards, you give me a chance to be on the team.

"That's a joke, right?" Coach Carter answered with an agitated look on his face.

"Well, let's see if it's a joke, coach," Emma said.

The boys on the team began to arrive and see what was happening.

"What the hell is Emma Townsend doing out here? And what is she doing putting on a pair of football shoes?" Ed Maguire said as he turned to look at the other players.

A crowd developed, and Coach Carter, smiling to himself, called to Donny Wilburn, the team's extra point holder. "Hey, Donnie, get over here and hold the ball for Emma. She's gonna try to kick the ball through the goalpost."

"I know, I know." Coach Carter said to Donnie. "Just hold the ball for her."

Coach Carter wasn't about to tell Emma that the *Cutrusville Tigers* football team had lost their past two games because of their kicker, Martin Planter. He had missed two easy field goals and, because of it, decided to quit the team.

"Hey, let's get this over with so we can get practice going." Coach Carter said impatiently.

Donnie set the ball on the thirty-yard line, and the next thing you heard was a loud "thud". The sound bounced off the side of the gym building, making everyone think a stick of dynamite exploded. The thud was Emma's foot hitting the ball as it hurled its way through the goalpost thirty yards away. Again, Donnie placed the ball on the thirty-yard line, and "boom," the ball went off Emma's foot again like a missile out of the space shuttles down in Cape Canaveral.

Coach Carter stood there with his mouth wide open. 'How in the hell could this be happening?' He wondered.

"How about one from forty yards, coach?" Emma yelled, with the same tone she had when she blasted the rednecks at the baseball tournament years back.

"You make it from there, and you're on the team." The coach announced as his jaw covered his Adam's apple. "And I don't give a rat's ass what anyone thinks about me having a girl on our team."

You'd be right if you guessed that she nailed it. That day, Emma became a member of the *Cutrus High Tigers*. Her dad sat in the stands boasting to all that his daughter kicked ass as she helped the Tigers go on to win the state championship.

Emma enrolled at the University of Florida and majored in Recreation. She met her future wife, Ellen Carmichael, and they eventually moved to Torrid Hills, where Emma had been offered the job as Director of Recreation. In his toast at their wedding, her dad announced with full confidence, "My daughter just proved to everyone that no matter what, she will help change the world."

5

The *Scotty Jones's Athletic Complex* ceremony was scheduled for the upcoming Saturday. It was a big day in Torrid Hills, and Emma and Sara scurried around the complex like the Queen of England was coming. Scotty Jones felt like he was that important in his blown-up, egotistical mind as he sat at *Andy's Bar and Grill,* regaling his cronies about his past accomplishments.

"Let's cut that grass like Alex Sumpter will cut Scotty Jones's hair today," Emma yelled at Tony Pulusie, the lawn maintenance guy. "You know damn well that Scotty will demand that Alex make him look like Brad Pitt. Not a hair out of place."

"It wasn't my idea," Emma said to Sara, who stood shaking her head in disbelief as maintenance workers, spiked with an overdose of adrenaline, picked up the tiniest bits of debris lying around. They looked a lot like the groundskeepers the day before The Masters golf tournament.

"Like I mentioned when you first arrived, Scotty Jones rules Torrid Hills." Emma moaned. "And whatever Scotty wants, Scotty gets. Did I tell you that it was his idea that he gets the field named after him?"

"You're kidding?" Sara said. "I guess you're right. His big head may not fit in the size of Texas. All this fuss here over one man seems like a farmer giving sirloin steak to his pigs."

Saturday morning rolled around, and Sara was up at the crack of dawn. Scotty Jones was probably wallowing in self-appreciation as the sun rose. Nary, a cloud was in sight. Sara's cell phone rang with Emma on the other line saying, "Time to get rolling. The Torrid Hills

High School band will be coming down Mulberry Street at 9:00 AM. We need to be at the park beforehand to give instructions to Scotty about what he needs to do. I asked him to meet us there at 8:30."

"That should be interesting," Sara said, chuckling. "I'll be there soon."

Sara, wanting to look her best for the day's ceremonies, put on her new pair of jeans and the University of Texas shirt and headed to the park. Upon arriving, she eyed Emma sitting on the bleachers with a man who appeared her father's age and another man considerably younger.

"Good morning, Sara," Emma said as Sara approached. "I want you to meet one of Torrid Hills' most famous citizens."

"*Scotty Jones.*" Scotty bellowed out in his usual condescending manner. "And this is my son, Arnold. And who would this fine-looking young lady be, Emma?"

"She is my new assistant, Sara Tobin," Emma replied.

"Pleased to meet you," Scotty said while Arnold sat there staring at Sara as if he had just seen the finest thing to come to Torrid Hills since Maddison Zachary won the state beauty pageant two years ago.

"And welcome to Torrid Hills," Scotty continued. "I suppose a nice-looking girl like you already has a boyfriend, but if not, I know someone available." He gestured toward Arnold.

Sara cringed and hoped her eyes didn't give away her contempt for Scotty's uncalled-for comment. She changed the subject quickly, saying, "It's nice to be working here in Torrid Hills. Congratulations on naming this park after you." she said, biting her tongue.

"Let's start this brief meeting by discussing what we need you to do for today's event Scotty," Emma said gingerly. Sensing Sara's irritation with Scotty's comment

For the next few minutes, Scotty stared into space as if bored. Cloud formations seemed more important to him than what Emma had to say. In the meantime, Sara couldn't help noticing Arnold fixated on the ground.

"Well, I say it's time to move out to the grandstand in centerfield," Emma said as the sound of the Torrid Hills High School band could be heard working its way down Mulberry Street toward the park.

The clattering sound of locals filling the seats in the infield gave witness to the significance of the event. Scotty sat straight in his seat, chest puffed out; you'd have thought he was the South's most crucial war hero about to receive the Medal of Honor.

"Welcome to today's event." Announced Rick Harris, Torrid Hills' newly elected mayor.

The event went on for over two hours.

Sitting in the back row, Sara eyed Arnold Jones, constantly peeking in her direction. She couldn't help but feel sorry for him after his father's embarrassing comments. She felt the urge to return a glance when she caught Arnold taking another peek. When their eyes met, Arnold looked like a turtle trying to hide his head beneath his collar. You might not call it love at first sight, but there was something trying to light a spark between the two. Sara giggled to herself, wondering if Arnold saw that she might be interested too.

6

With the ceremony over and Scotty putting his self-regard in cruise control, Torrid Hills again became its boring southern self on this quiet Spring Day.

Emma and Sara finished cleaning the park and took a break at one of the park's picnic tables. The darkening Maple trees stood motionless in the background as they wished a tiny breeze would relieve them of the unusual stillness hovering over the park.

"You know what, Sara?" Emma said, leaning over toward Sara as if she were about to tell her a secret.

"What's that?" Sara replied.

"We should go down to *Andy's* and award ourselves a few cold beers. What do you think?" Emma said, pleading as if she were a schoolgirl trying to sneak out of school.

"Well, I sure could use a cold one after this long day." Sara sighed with a sense of joy.

Emma's cheeks curled up on the ride to Andy's as she leaned toward Sara and said, "So what did you think of Scotty's son, Arnold? Kind of cute, isn't he?"

Without warning, the red complexion glowing on Sara's face turned even brighter. Sure, the sun had been bearing down at the park, but this skin tone change came from within.

"Uh-oh," claimed Emma, hinting that she had hit a nerve with Sara. "Do I sense a bit of someone attracted to someone?"

"No," Sara said sheepishly and not too convincingly. "I'll admit he's cute, but I could never imagine anything more. His father sealed that deal with his offensive comment."

"I agree." Emma reacted hurriedly. "So, let's drop that stupid thought. Sorry, I even brought it up."

"Is *Andy's* the only place in town where people hang out?" Sara asked.

"Well, there's *Hanagan's*, but it struggles to compete because there aren't many Irish people in this town to support it," Emma replied.

Andy's Bar and Grill appeared like your typical local hangout from the outside. It used to be called *Andy's on the Water.* The funny thing is that there is no water outside the bar. According to locals, it had dried up after a long drought several years earlier and never returned.

Grungy-looking would be one way to describe the *"Andy's"* sign. It looked like it hadn't been touched in years. The Miller Lite sign, annoyingly blinking on and off, made it seem like it was the only beer they served inside.

The place was packed with well-wishers from the day's earlier event honoring Scotty. Entering Andy's, Emma and Sara squinted their eyes almost closed, trying to adjust their pupils from the bright sun outside. They spotted a table in the corner and immediately sat looking around at the patrons. A voice came from nowhere saying, "Great job today, ladies." The voice was Al Supries, the barber who had cut Scotty's hair.

"Did I do good enough to make Scotty look presentable?" Al asked in a manner to suggest he was looking for affirmation of a job well done, not to mention an invite to join Emma and Sara.

"Absolutely," Emma said as she looked around the room, hoping Al would sense he wasn't invited to sit at the table.

"Well, great." Al anxiously said, bending his head, looking like the last kid chosen for his little league team.

"Hey, there's Ellen," Emma shouted as Ellen entered the bar. Ellen Danner was one of Torrid Hills' commissioners who encouraged the other commissioners to hire Emma. "Come sit with us, Ellen. I want you to meet my new assistant." Emma said with a sense of pride.

"Hi, Sara," Ellen said as she sat at the table. "I already know you from everything Emma has told me."

"I hope they have been positive," Sara responded.

"If Emma talked about me as nicely as she talks about you, I'd be delighted," Ellen stated as the curl in her lips tightened.

Arnold Jones, in the meantime, and a group of friends happened to be sitting on the other side of the room downing their beers like they had a contest going.

Mark Tanner joined the group as he usually does after work. He and Arnold had grown up a block from each other, and from day one, Mark would hang out at Arnold's house. His parents never got along and would put Mark in the middle of their arguments. Finally, when Mark's father threatened to kill Mark's mother, Mark left the house and lived in a one-room apartment at age eighteen. Arnold could empathize with Mark because his house atmosphere wasn't much better. It's why they got along so much for all those years.

"So, would you look at that fine thing sitting over at the table with Emma Thomson and Ellen Tanner?" Mark nodded to the group. "Damn, she's hot. Who the hell is she? I got to get to know her."

"You're a little late, my friend," Arnold said, half-jokingly but perhaps more seriously than he let on.

"How so?" Mark questioned.

"I met her this morning at the ceremony for my dad. She's the new assistant recreation director who works with Emma. I sure would like to get to know her better."

"Well, I'm giving you one week. I'm moving in if you haven't won her over by then. I know she couldn't resist me with all my charm."

Ellen said to Sara at Sara's table, "So why did you decide to move to Torrid Hills, Sara?"

"It's a long story, but suffice it to say that my family decided it was time to move on from Texas."

"Well, on behalf of the city, I'd like to welcome you and your family."

After a couple more beers, and a few sly glances toward Arnold's table, Sara said, "Well, I guess it's time to head home. I'm worn out from this long day.

7

A subjugated Arnold was twenty-four years old when he decided he couldn't take it anymore. Living at home had become a nightmare. Fearful of upsetting Scotty, Arnold cautiously announced that he had just acquired a new job as the night clerk at the newly remodeled *Torrid Hills Inn*. With the job came a free room. And the free room provided the perfect alibi to get away.

"You'll be back here within a month." Scotty said in his usual belittling tone.

"Maybe." Arnold responded.

Feeling like a ton of bricks had been taken off his shoulders, Arnold began his new job at the Inn. Though escaping the constant belittling while living at home, he was still unable to explain the ceaseless feeling of depression that wore on him day….and night. He decided it was time he should see someone who might help. Knowing the humiliation he would face from others who chided individuals who would seek help for mental health issues, he decided to make an appointment with Dr. Leslie Monroe in Greensboro, forty miles away.

"Dr. Monroe will see you now." The receptionist said.

Within fifteen minutes of conversation between the two, Dr. Monroe stated that it seemed Arnold's most prevalent problem centered around his childhood and relationship with his parents.

"Have you had problems related to your parents?" Dr. Monroe questioned. Arnold suddenly felt panic and gripped the armrest of his chair.

"I'd say yes," Arnold replied as his palms began to sweat, fearful of saying the next line. "For the most part, it goes back to when I played little league."

"How so?" Dr. Monroe asked as she cocked her head to the side.

"I just was never able to please my parents. They would always criticize me when I made mistakes. They would tell me at times that I would never amount to anything. One time they told me that I was an embarrassment. That really hurt. I was only ten years old at the time. And as I tell you this now, it hurts as bad as the first time those words came out of their mouth."

"Both of your parents made these hurtful comments?" asked Dr. Monroe.

"Oh yes. But it was mostly by my father." Arnold told the psychologist.

"He would never let up. He had been a star athlete in his day, and he couldn't understand why I wasn't one too."

The floodgates seemed to open as Arnold spent the next part of their session describing one event after another where the abuse took place. The outpour of his emotions let loose like water coming out of a drainpipe after a rainstorm.

"Our time is up for today, Arnold." Dr. Monroe said, sensing she had depleted all the emotional energy Arnold had remaining in his body. "I think we can get to the bottom of your problem, but it will take time. You have opened the door to what might be causing your depression, but we are only scratching the surface. I need to know more about it. In the meantime, try not to let your mind go backward, thinking about the apparent abuses you have faced. We'll deal with them as we progress."

Arnold left the psychologist's office feeling emotionally healthier, like a young tree in the sun. He was on a path he had never traveled, and for some reason, the path made him feel good. As he rode back to

Torrid Hills, his mind began drifting. Within moments, the memory of Sara sitting at *Andy's* a few days before popped into his head and made him feel jittery. His stomach churned as his insides began vibrating. Why, he wondered to himself? Was she *that* attractive? Whatever it was, he was determined to find the answer.

Arriving back in Torrid Hills, Arnold decided to stop by *Andy's* for a beer. Jeff Jenkins, his best friend from high school, was seated at the bar.

"S'up, big guy?" Arnold yelled as he grabbed Jeff around the chest with both hands, almost knocking Jeff's beer on the floor.

"Well, if it ain't my boy, Arnold Jones," Jeff said, turning with his arms out as if to hug the world. "Where the hell you been hidin', brother?"

"Got me a new job," Arnold replied, his chest puffing out as if at ease with the world.

"Where's that?" Jeff asked quizzically.

"Torrid Hills Inn." Arnold answered timidly, fearing the perception of him having a less than erudite form of employment might result in Jeff looking down on him.

"So, what do you do there, manage the place?" Jeff came back with a sly grin.

"Not yet," Arnold answered quickly. Then changing the subject, "What's going on with you these days?"

As Jeff was about to answer, the door to *Andy's* opened, and in walked Sara Tobin, all alone.

"Who the hell is that fine-looking thing?" Jeff said, turning his head toward the door. Arnold almost choked on his beer.

With his voice sounding two octaves above middle C, Arnold, under his breath, said, "That's Sara. I forget her last name."

"Why are you so nervous?" Jeff chided. "You act like you're a married man who just got caught sneaking out of the house."

"I met her the other day at my dad's event." Arnold responded. "That's all I know."

"Well, hell, you can't just sit here and pretend she doesn't exist." Jeff admonished. "Get over there, say hello, and then invite her to come over and let you buy her a beer. C'mon, man." Jeff demanded.

"You think I should?" Arnold said. Sounding like a third-grade timid boy afraid to sit next to a girl he liked.

"Get over there before I push you out of this barstool!" Jeff insisted as if he were a drill sergeant ordering the troops to battle.

With that, Arnold left his barstool and walked gingerly over to the table where Sara was sitting. As he walked, the door flew open, and in walked Cathy Ellerson.

Seeing her, Sara yelled, "Cathy, I'm over here."

Sara and Cathy had met at the Torrid Hills *Bowlerama* not long after Sara and her family had moved to town. Cathy had been signed onto the Tobin's team in the *Bowlerama* adult league. When needed, she volunteered to work in the concession stand selling hot dogs, Cokes, or whatever goodies people get a hankering for at bowling events. She had just moved to Torrid Hill two months prior and wanted to go out to meet people. She and Sara became fast friends. They were both single, and neither was in any hurry to change that status.

Poor Arnold found himself stuck between a rock and a hard place halfway between the bar and Sara's table. He panicked, wondering how to get out of the dilemma. He kept walking, pretending he was on his way to the restroom. As he walked toward Sara, he nodded a perfunctory "hello."

As Cathy approached Sara's table, she saw Arnold heading in the same direction and assumed they were there together. "Hey, Arnold. Haven't seen you since we met that day at 7-11. What brings you and Sara here? I didn't know you two knew each other."

Arnold gulped but got out, "Hi Cathy. Good to see you again. I was just on my way to the restroom, but I did meet Sara a few days ago at my dad's park affair".

As he kept walking, he whispered to himself, "Damnit," thinking he had just missed his big chance. But all was not lost as Cathy saved the day. At least for today. Walking his way back to the bar from the restroom, Cathy motioned to Arnold, "Hey, if you're all alone, why not sit down and join us?"

"My friend Jeff and I have been over at the bar, but if you don't mind, I'll ask him to join too."

"Sure, why not." Cathy said.

The four of them sat talking and laughing for hours. Sara told them about how she and her family ended up in Torrid Hills after her father left his practice in Norland, Texas. They all talked about their high school experiences, and Sara, Cathy, and Jeff boasted of their athletic abilities that earned them state records, team captains, or college scholarships. With each story being told, it felt like a knife going through Arnold's side. Remembering the days of being ridiculed and humiliated became too much. Without any fanfare, he quietly stood up and announced that he was late for work and would see them all later. He gave one last look at Sara for the night. She was smiling at him. It gave him hope that they would be seeing each other a little more often.

Sara sat thinking to herself, 'Was this serendipitous moment about to lead to something life-changing?' She had been thinking about Arnold since the ceremony at the park. He seemed to like her, and she thought she just might feel the same.

8

"Want a cup of coffee, Sara?" Emma asked as she walked into the office that Monday morning.

"Sounds good to me," Sara replied, ready to start the week wide awake.

"When it's not raining cats and dogs outside, I sure like Fall weather in North Carolina," Sara told Emma as she took the first delightful sip of coffee. Looking out the window, she said, "Those ballfields out there sure bring back the days I spent playing soccer as a kid."

"How old were you when you first began playing?" Emma asked.

"I was six," Sara answered. "But then I quit when I was eleven."

"Eleven?" Emma blurted out in disbelief. "That's an early age to quit. I guess you figured you'd never get a chance to play, so you quit, huh?"

"Oh no." Sara said, "I was one of the best players on the team. It's kind of a long story."

"Well, with how it's raining, we're not going anywhere." Emma said as she crossed her arms and leaned in with anticipation, wanting to hear Sara's story.

"Okay, if you really want to hear it," Sara said, taking a deep breath.

"My best friend Anita Thornapple and I were inseparable since first grade. I was either sleeping at her house, or she was at mine all the time. We were in the same class every year, and then we both

43

decided to sign up for the soccer program at the Norland rec department.

When soccer season began, Anita and I ended up being the best players on the team. Our coach, Mr. Allison, loved the way we played. He would ask us to stay after practice so he could show us special plays for us to score more goals. He'd even offer to drive us home, so our parents wouldn't have to take time from work to drive us. We were getting so good our team made it to the regional playoffs."

"Impressive," Emma interjected.

"We liked Mr. Allison. So did our parents. He worked at the power and electric company in Norland. Every now and then, my parents would invite him over for dinner. He would buy presents for needy kids in the community at Christmas, making people think he could do no wrong. As far as everyone knew, or so he told everybody, his wife had died in a car wreck several years earlier. He had no kids, so to keep himself occupied, he volunteered to coach the soccer team."

"I feel like this is taking a dark turn." Emma commented.

"Yeah," Sara sighed. "About halfway through the season, I came down with the flu. I was so sick, with a 102 temperature, my mom took me to the hospital. I stayed there for three days. I was so weak that I couldn't attend school or soccer practice for a week. Coach Allison, however, insisted that Anita keep staying after practice.

One day, out of nowhere, Anita called me with her voice quivering, telling me she was quitting. I was stunned and kept asking her why, but she started crying and said she didn't want to talk about it and hung up on me.

My thoughts were swirling so much that I didn't know which way to turn. It was as if my brain had stopped working. It wasn't like Anita at all.

I decided to go over to her house. When I got there, the police were there talking to her parents. I went to her room, and when she saw me, she started crying again.

I tried to stay calm and just waited for her to talk. After what seemed like an eternity, she began to tell me what had happened. She called Coach Allison a monster. She said he was driving her home after practice and stopped to pick up some beer at the convenience store. Then tried to give her one of them. She was only eleven! When she wouldn't drink any, he drank both down right there in the parking lot. Then instead of taking her to her house, he took her to some warehouse district and parked the car. When she told him she wanted to go home, she said he got agitated and opened another beer. Then he began to open the zipper in his pants and asked her if she would like to see what he had hidden inside. She said she tried to get out of the car but was locked in. Then she started crying and banging on the window. Thankfully, a man came out of the warehouse and looked to see what was happening. She said he rushed over, and when Coach Allison tried to pull away, the man stood in front of the car and pulled out a gun. He ordered Coach Allison to open the door and let Anita out. She said that she was so scared she had peed her pants. It was a big deal in our town, and Coach Allison got arrested.

To make it even worse, the soccer league simply apologized and asked another parent to coach the team." *

"Unfortunately, that's not too different from how we handle things here," Emma remarked. "I'm sorry you and your friend had to go through that."

"Yeah, after that, I decided to quit soccer along with Anita," Sara replied.

As she stared out the window, Sara wondered what exactly Emma meant by 'not too different' when it came to handling situations of abuse at the rec department. But she didn't ask.

*More than 1 in 4 current or former student-athletes reported being sexually assaulted in youth sports programs.

9

"HAAAAY, SARA!" Cathy blared out as if she were speaking through one of those megaphones that cheerleaders use at football games. It's a wonder all the "Sara's" living in Torrid Hills didn't think someone was calling to them.

"Damn, that girl has a loud voice," Larry La Gore, the maintenance man, complained to Sara as they continued discussing the field condition for Saturday's football game.

With Sara being more than a hundred yards away, it was par for the course for Cathy to be screaming at the top of her lungs instead of walking over toward her. People around Torrid Hills got used to Cathy's undignified way of being. But they liked her just the same.

Cathy moved to Torrid Hills from Alfred, Pennsylvania. Her parents were divorced, and she wanted nothing to do with her father. He got caught stealing tires at a dealership in Alfred and selling them online. They sentenced him to one year in jail. That's when she decided she had had enough and planned to move "anywhere," as she put it. "Anywhere" ended up being Torrid Hills.

Being twenty-five years old, Cathy had not been lucky in love. She had been married and divorced two times. The first was to Albert Willis, an airline pilot who took off with a flight attendant after four months and settled in Chicago. The other guy, Ralph Redley, raised turkeys in West Virginia. Cathy caught the turkey farmer in bed with another farmer's daughter. Myrna Monaghan, who worked at the post office with her, swore Cathy was always in love with love.

"I'll be over in a minute," Sara yelled back to Cathy as she finished her conversation with Larry LaGore. Larry, a likable guy, was the head maintenance man for *Scotty Jones Park*.

Sara began feeling at ease in her new role as Assistant Director of Recreation. One thing that troubled her with the position was that she would oversee giving out permits for the various fields year-round. In Torrid Hills, the rec department determined who could or couldn't lease the fields. In spring, little league baseball groups practically occupied the whole complex with their different levels of age groups. In the fall, football and soccer groups battled out who got what fields and when. "A fucking nightmare!" Emma called it.

In June of the previous year, a *Grandstand Sports Travel Teams* representative approached Emma about renting the fields for travel teams in all sports.

"So you're telling me you will pay our recreation department for using the fields?" Emma asked with a bit of skepticism.

"Yes, ma'am," the representative said. "We aim to have the best athletes in Torrid Hills emerge and go on to college scholarships or the pros."

"And I guess the parents who sign their kids up for your program will have to pay?"

"Yes, they will." the rep stated. "We will provide professional coaches who will need to be compensated."

"Will the families that sign on be guaranteed their child will get a college scholarship?"

"Well, we can't guarantee that, Ms. Townsend."

"What happens to all the other kids who are not so good? Where will they go to play if we give you the fields?" Emma asked, starting to feel upset by the thought that most of the kids in Torrid Hills would not qualify and be left with nowhere to play.

"Well, if you want Torrid Hills to develop world-class athletes, that's how it will be."

"That's the way it won't be, sir." Emma fired back at the representative. "All kids in Torrid Hills deserve to play on our fields. Sports are more than trying to make it for scholarships or the pros. If they're good enough, talent scouts will hear about them. They don't need your program to succeed." *

Sara had secured the rec job in Torrid Hills at the right time since football had won over the rights for the best field, while soccer got "the crumbs," according to the soccer league president.

With her conversation with Larry over, Sara jogged across the field toward Cathy, and as she jogged, her huffing and puffing sounded like the last contestant of a twenty-six-mile marathon. "Damn, I'm out of shape," she said, gasping away.

"What's up, Cathy?" Sara said, catching her breath.

"I just heard that there's a Halloween party Saturday night at the *Torrid Hills Inn*. You know, the one where Arnold works. It's a dress-up Halloween costume event and looks like fun. You in?" Cathy pleaded as if her whole future love life depended on it.

"Why not?" Sara replied. "I was beginning to think there was some ordinance against socializing in this town."

Saturday night rolled around when Cathy called Sara, "Hey, why don't I pick you up around nine-thirty, and we can go together?"

"I was hoping you'd drive since you're not a drinker," Sara replied. "Not that I pound them down, but you know what I mean."

"What did you decide to wear?" Cathy asked Sara. "I hope it's not some clown suit where no one will recognize you."

"Oh no," Sara said. "I decided to be a French maid."

"Oooh, sexy!" Cathy said with a devilish grin. "I know what you're up to."

"Hey, I gotta let these people know that the town rec director is not some grown-up tomboy," Sara responded with a sly smile.

"Are you sure the 'these people' isn't about 'one person' by the name Arnold Jones?" Cathy said teasingly to Sara.

"Maybe it is, maybe it isn't," Sara responded coyly, looking down at the unbuttoned collar on her outfit, making sure the uplift bra accentuated her breasts.

The two arrived at the *Torrid Hills Inn*, and who would be standing at the entrance? None other than the man himself, Arnold Jones.

Martin Tolner, the hotel's owner, put Arnold in charge of the party for the evening. Arnold wanted to give the impression that the Halloween gathering was his event. Standing at the entrance would do that. Surely, he wouldn't want to be seen standing behind the front desk registering people for rooms. Leonard Terrill, his assistant, would handle that job for the night.

Arnold decided to dress as a medieval king, crown and all. It fits perfectly with his desire to let the attendees (those who didn't know him) think this was his event, not to mention…. his hotel.

As Sara and Cathy walked toward the hotel's front entrance, Arnold eyed Sara. His mouth dropped open like a trapped door, looking like he was opening wide for the dentist. The sight of Sara, and her alluring outfit, caused Arnold to feel light-headed and think, "Damn, she looks hot. What do I say to her? Do I play it cool?" The thoughts ran through his head like a speeding train as Sara got closer and closer.

Then, the moment of Zen. "Hi, Arnold," Sara said as she and Cathy reached the front door.

Arnold's knees buckled. The sweetness of Sara's voice felt like listening to the voice of an angel.

"G-good evening, ladies." Arnold stammered, trying to brace himself as his heart beat so loud he feared he might pass out. "I hope you have a good time tonight." was all he could get out.

Practically the whole town of Torrid Hills came to the party. Even Scotty Jones. Spotting Arnold at the entrance, Scotty, like a tiger grabbing its prey for dinner, forcibly pulled his wife, Martha, by the arm and looked for the side entrance.

"What are you doing? Martha yelled at Scotty.

"Didn't you see who stood out front greeting people like some damn fool?"

Meanwhile, Sara and Cathy walked around the ballroom, looking at all the different outfits. A few of the womenfolk of Torrid Hills gathered in the corner like the mistresses of morality, casting evil eyes toward Sara and her exposed bosom. Sara catching their glances, said to Cathy, "Let them eat their hearts out."

Cathy, not about to let those ladies get away with their snide looks, walked toward the group as if she were about to scold a spoiled child and grumbled, "Can I get you ladies a shot of bourbon? You look like you need it."

Upon watching Cathy let loose on them, Sara lost control of the beer she was sipping, and it flew out her mouth like champagne bursting out of a bottle.

"Damn, you're a crazy girl," Sara said, laughing at Cathy.

An hour into the event, Sara told Cathy she might step outside for a breath of fresh air.

"You don't fool me. I know where you're going." Cathy said with a devilish grin.

"He's probably lonely out there," Sara said, her eyes fluttering like a butterfly. Cathy was already focused on Ian Delatonte, who she had her eyes on since she saw him at the Beacon Street Market the previous week. As Sara neared the front door, she stopped in her tracks. She spotted Scotty approaching Arnold.

"When the hell are you gonna get a real job, Arnold?" Sara could hear Scotty yelling. "Why are you standing out here looking like a buffoon? You're as embarrassing out here as much as you were playing little league. A loser, a loser, a loser, is what you are." Scotty said, screaming into Arnold's face.

Arnold stood staring at Scotty, shattered by his comments, just as he had always been for the past twenty-seven years.

As Scotty walked away, Sara felt a boundless empathy for Arnold. She approached him as he stood there with his head down and his cloak drooped sadly over his shoulders. "I'm sorry, Arnold. I stumbled into your conversation with your father as I came out for some fresh air.

"Conversation?" Arnold replied like steam coming from a pressure cooker. "I'm just sorry you had to hear it."

"That had to be painful for you to be talked to like that," Sara said to him.

Arnold was embarrassed. "It's been that way all my life, Sara." Tears began to form in his eyes. "That's the way he is. I just don't know why. What did I do wrong to deserve his wrath?" Arnold cried out, with his head shaking in bewilderment.

"You did nothing wrong, Arnold," Sara said. "This is your father's issue, not yours. Maybe he's bipolar. My mom is a psychologist, and I've heard her talk a lot about family abuse. One thing is for sure, it isn't your fault. But I'm sure it's excruciating, though."

"I feel better already," Arnold said as he looked at Sara, wishing the moment would never end. He wondered if he should mention his visit with the psychologist.

"Do you think we could talk some more sometime?" Arnold asked Sara as the thought of a giant eraser swept across his mind and, with it, the ugliest experiences of the past vanishing.

"Sure, I'm at the field almost every day. Just call me, and we'll get together soon." Sara answered, then smiled and walked back inside.

What felt like one of the worst times of his life quickly turned into one of the best moments for Arnold.

Bowing his head, clenching his fist, and pumping it to the ground, Arnold said under his breath, *"Yes!"* He couldn't wait to make the phone call.

The travel team phenomenon has replaced recreational league play in many local recreation programs.

10

Rocking back and forth in his chair, Arnold had a feeling in his stomach like a lump of lead. "Pick me up," the cell phone staring at him kept saying. At least, that's what he kept hearing from the voice inside his head. "Come on, chicken," reverberated around his brain like an iron ball inside a pinball machine. Finally, he took a deep breath and picked up the phone with his hands shaking so bad, the phone almost slipped as he dialed Sara's number. "Please pick up, please pick up," he said into the phone for what seemed a lifetime.

"Hi, this is Sara." The voice on the other end said to the relief of Arnold, bringing his heart rate from 200 down to 70.

"Hi, this is Arnold," He replied. You'd have thought you were listening to one of those commercials on the radio where the guy talks so fast you can't understand what he's saying, "I just wanted to follow up on your offer to set up a time to meet." Not waiting for Sara to respond, Arnold quickly said, "How about we meet at *Morty's* for lunch tomorrow?"

"I think I heard you right," Sara replied, catching her breath and trying to keep up with Arnold's fast-paced request. "You're asking me to go to lunch tomorrow at *Morty's*, right?"

"Now, if you can't make it, I understand," Arnold replied, squirming in his chair as if he had an itch on his butt.

"No, no," Sara responded gingerly. "I'd love to meet you. I get an hour for lunch every day."

Arnold was beside himself as he said, "See you tomorrow at noon sharp."

"Why did I say, 'noon sharp'?" Arnold said to himself as he hung up the phone. "She probably thinks I'm some kind of nerd. No one says to someone, "Noon sharp," especially when you're meeting for your first date. Wait, is this a date? Should I call her back and apologize?"

It's safe to say that Arnold coming off his phone call with Sara made him a little more than nervous. Getting to sleep that night was another issue.

It was 6:30 am when Arnold's phone rang. He tossed and turned so much the night before the sheets on his bed were almost frayed. Today was the big day.

"Hello," Arnold answered, wondering who would be calling him at 6:30 in the morning on his day off.

"Arnold," the voice said. "This is Allen Trumble. We have some disgruntled guests who want to meet at 11:00 to discuss their complaints about the room. You need to go down to the front desk then and handle it. Sorry, I know this is your day off, but that's the way it goes in the hotel business."

Allen was Arnold's boss, and like all bosses, you don't want to make them unhappy.

"Ok, I'll meet with them," Arnold said, forgetting his lunch meeting with Sara for the moment.

Morty's was only twenty minutes from *Torrid Hills Inn*, so he figured he could make it by noon with no problem. That is, with no hitch.

Arnold left his room at the hotel and headed to the front desk at 10:45, anxious to get the dispute with the guest handled as soon as possible.

"Nothing in the room worked." The disgruntled guest complained. "I want a full refund."

"Well, the manager has to approve," Arnold replied.

"Well, get the damn manager," the guest said, as the need for an anger manager might be needed along with the hotel manager.

"I'll have to call him," Arnold said. "Hold on."

"Mr. Trumble stepped outside and will be back in a minute Arnold." The voice on the phone said.

Arnold began to sweat, and that empty pit in his stomach returned. It was now 11:10, and Mr. Trumble was still outside. He didn't need this aggravation. This was a big day for him, and he didn't want anything to screw it up. It was now 11:20, and Mr. Trumble still hadn't returned.

"Screw it," Arnold said, bordering on a panic attack. "Give him a full refund and tell Mr. Trumble I had to make an emergency decision without him."

Now 11:30, with twenty minutes to *Morty's,* Arnold felt a sigh of relief. Jumping in his beat-up Chevy, he took a deep breath, and with hands clasped in prayer and eyes closed, he said to himself, *"Let's make this a great day."*

As he turned the key to turn on the car engine, he heard a sound no car owner wanted to hear, a *"click, click, click"* kept bouncing back from the engine like an annoying old-time typewriter. The battery was dead.

"NOOOOOOOOO!" Arnold screamed so loud Ann Tangier, the lady at the front desk, came running out saying, "What happened, Arnold?"

Too shocked to answer, Arnold jumped out of the car and took off for *Morty's.* You'd have thought a swarm of angry bees was after him as he flew down the road, never thinking he could have called Sara to tell her of his dilemma. Running at a pace that even his father Scotty would have admired, he was about a mile from *Morty's* when he eyed a car coming in his direction. It was Cathy. Waving his arms frantically as if he were being attacked by a herd of wolves, Cathy's car stopped and in jumped Arnold. It was now 12:15.

You'd have thought a swarm of angry bees was after him as he raced down the road, never thinking that he could have called Sara to tell her of his dilemma. Running at a pace that even his father Scotty would have admired, he was about a mile from *Morty's* when he eyed a car coming in his direction. It was Cathy. Waving his arms frantically as if he were being attacked by a herd of wolves, Cathy's car stopped and in jumped Arnold. It was now 12:15.

"Oh, thank heaven it was you. I'm supposed to meet Sara at noon at *Morty's*. Do you think there's any chance she will still be there?" Arnold's heart began sinking like a ship going underwater.

"Let's hope so!" Cathy said, stepping on the gas.

Meanwhile, at twelve o'clock, Sara sat nervously glancing at the clock on the wall at *Morty's*, anxious for the next few moments when Arnold would arrive. She felt disappointed, like a huge wave knocking her to the shore when the clock's hand dropped to 12:15. At 12:20, she said to Morty behind the bar, "Sorry, guess my guest got tied up." She walked out the door feeling dumped by someone she hardly knew. With her head down, she walked to her car. Suddenly, around the corner, she saw Cathy's car racing toward her. When she reached the parking lot, Cathy's car came to a stop so abruptly that she spun around almost in a complete circle, nearly running over Sara.

"IT'S NOT HIS FAULT" Cathy screamed at about the volume she reached at the park the other day.

"Oh, I'm so sorry, Sara," Arnold said, trying to atone for failing to attend their lunch meeting. "Please forgive me."

"Just tell him to quit groveling," Cathy yelled in her own devilish manner, trying to soften the moment.

"Well, I guess after that, I have to," Sara said. "Now give me the short version 'cause I gotta get to work."

"Would it be too much to ask if you could drop me off back at the Inn? I think you'd still have enough time left in your hour lunch, and I can tell you the story along the way." Arnold pleaded.

"Damn, you're testing my patience," Sara replied with a grin on her face that belied any sense of irritation.

"I hope you two get along better the next time," Cathy said, razzing the two of them like opponents at a college football game.

"We'll try!" Sara answered as Arnold climbed into the front seat. She winked at Cathy with a gleeful smile.

11

On the drive back to the office, Sara's cell phone rang with Emma on the other end squirming in her chair like a nervous fish.

"We got us a problem, Sara." Emma said, making Sara think she had returned late from the "almost" lunch date.

"Sorry if I was late coming back from lunch. I can explain." Sara said apologetically.

"I wish that were it," Emma responded. "The problem is with the football program. At this morning's game, Eldredge Mcloughlin, the quarterback of the *Outters* football team, was carted off to the hospital."

"Oh, no! What happened?" Sara asked with anticipation of something serious.

"From what I've been told, it was the game's last quarter. Eldridge was carrying the ball and running around the end toward the goal line when Donnie Welbring on the other team nailed him with a vicious hit. He was laying on the ground, unable to move, when one of the coaches, Brocky Leonard, tried to pick him up."

"That's the worst thing you can do. I learned that during my first year in *First Aid and Safety* in college." Sara said.

"It gets worse," Emma said with a knot in her stomach. "Try to picture this. Brocky, who is all but eighteen years old, decides to be a first responder. Without any first responder training! He tells Eldridge to stand up. As he struggles to stand, he then asks Eldridge where it hurts. Eldridge says that his shoulder hurts "real bad." Brocky then decides that the problem is that Eldridge has the ball at the top of the shoulder knocked out of the socket. At that point, Brocky tells the other coaches that when he played, he remembers one coach," "popping" another player's shoulder back in place. The other coaches said to do it cause they wanted him back in the game. With that, Brocky tells Eldridge to raise his arm. He then puts a fist directly into Eldridge's armpit, like making a fulcrum. Then biting his teeth, He pushes down as hard as he can on Eldridge's wrist. As soon as he does, Eldridge screams in pain and passes out on the ground. Blood is coming out in the middle of Eldridge's arm between the shoulder and the elbow. At that point, they started yelling to call an ambulance. The ambulance arrived and took Eldridge to the hospital. Since it happened on our field, I have to go to the hospital to see the extent of his injury. Why don't you meet me there, Sara." *

Sara drove to the hospital, pulling in almost simultaneously with Emma. Also pulling into the parking area were Eldridge's mom and dad.

"Is he okay" Eldridge's mom hollered to Emma as she feverishly jumped out of her car?

"I sure hope so," Emma said, not wanting to commit to anything as the four rushed to the emergency room.

By coincidence, Sara's dad was the doctor in attendance at the hospital when Eldridge was admitted. He would be the one to operate on Eldridge's arm.

After waiting almost two hours, Dr. Tobin came out and was surprised to see Sara waiting with the others. He called Eldridge's parents to talk privately about his condition.

Not long after, Eldridge's parents walked out of Dr. Tobin's office.

"How is he?" Sara asked her dad.

"I'm afraid I'm not at liberty to discuss Eldridge's condition." Dr. Tobin said to Sara and Emma.

"But *we* can." Eldridge's mother said. "Eldridge had a compound fracture due to the stupidity of having a kid diagnose his injury. And a rec department that would allow untrained people out there who don't have a clue how to deal with injuries!"

"You'll be hearing from our lawyer." Eldridge's father announced.

Emma and Sara stood stunned at the thought of being sued. "Could they go after us, too?" Sara asked Emma.

"I guess we're gonna find out," Emma replied, looking into space.

When five o'clock rolled around, Sara beat it out the door. Emma had told her to ask her father about the situation. She hoped he was able to divulge any information legally.

Once Sara's dad arrived home, she wasted no time asking, "I know you can't tell me any medical details, but can you tell me how it happened?"

"Well, in general, here's how these things can happen, hypothetically speaking," Jeff said to Sara as she sat on the edge of her chair.

"First, make a fist with your left hand, Sara. Now, put the fist under your right armpit with the fingers in your left hand facing toward you. That makes the point of the fulcrum the biggest. Got it? Next, slowly push your right fist toward your right hip. Feels a little hard for your fist to reach your right hip, right? That's the fulcrum. So, when someone does that to a person whose arm is *already* broken halfway between the elbow and the shoulder, guess what happens? The arm breaks even more, and if someone pushes it hard enough, the bone goes through the skin, causing a compound fracture and bleeding."

"That's horrible," Sara thought, becoming embittered by the thought that, indirectly, her rec department was at fault for never

63

questioning the football team's ability to provide first aid in the case of injury.

"If you want my opinion, Emma, we need to do something to protect the kids playing on our facilities from things like this happening again." Sara cautiously said.

"I agree, but what do you suggest? Emma questioned Sara.

"We need to make it a requirement that any organization wanting to use our facilities must have a qualified first aid person in attendance at all practice and games," Sara said emphatically.

"Let's do it," Emma said.

Sara couldn't wait to get to work to meet with Emma the following morning. When she walked in, Emma was sitting in her office with her first cup of coffee. Looking out the window, wondering how the recent football event was the first of its kind to happen. 'Why weren't we prepared?' she thought.

"I need to call Alvin Gross, the city attorney," Emma said as Sara walked into the room.

"Good idea," Sara responded

"Hi, Alvin Gross, here." The voice on the phone said.

"This is Emma Thompson at the rec department, Alvin. We had an incident on our football field where one of the players was injured. I realize it's a bit early, but I wanted you to know that the parents of the injured player indicated that they planned to sue everyone involved. My question is whether the rec department or even me and my assistant can be held liable for the injury if it occurred on our facility?"

"I'll have to look into it, Emma," Alvin replied. "I'm not so sure the department and its employees are liable, but I can assure you that someone out there is going to pay. Let's just hope that we find you clear in this instance. Did you make the football league that uses the facility sign a waiver that would indemnify the department? Regardless, I suggest you develop a training program for all those leagues that use the town's facilities. It would show people that your intent is to give the volunteers the information they need to help prevent and deal with any injuries that occur in the future. That would show due diligence."

Emma and Sara breathed a sigh of relief, albeit a little early to be off the hook. But it did make the rec department wake up to the fact that in the future, anyone wanting to use the facilities could not do so without being trained in making things safe for everyone...especially the kids in Torrid Hills.

This story was told by a former youth league football coach in Indiana.

12

A buzz went off on Sara's phone. It was a text from Arnold saying, "I've got an idea. How about I make up for my screw-up by inviting you to dinner tonight?" A buzz also went off in Sara's heart. She hadn't been on a date since she left Norland. She liked Arnold and hoped it might be the start of something that led to much more than dinner dates.

"Sounds like a great idea to me." Sara texted back. "Just tell me the time, and I'll be ready."

"Pick you up at 6 PM at your house." Arnold texted back, never thinking this would be the first time he'd meet Sara's parents. A tingling went off in his stomach, but it was more because he had scheduled a meeting with Dr. Monroe in Greensboro at 1 PM.

On the drive to Greensboro, Arnold wondered how long the sessions with Dr. Monroe would last before he felt relief from his father's abusive behavior. Maybe Sara could provide better relief than Dr. Monroe, he mused.

"Good afternoon, Arnold." Dr. Monroe said as she welcomed Arnold to her office. "You seem quite cheery today."

"Well, to be honest, Dr. Monroe, I have a date this evening," Arnold revealed, pressing his lips together to keep from smiling.

Dr. Monroe smiled and said, "That's great to hear. So, let's get started. Have a seat."

With prompting, Arnold began to describe some of the situations that had occurred in his childhood.

"The one that hurt the most was when I was playing baseball." He began.

"How old were you at the time?" Dr. Monroe asked.

"Nine," Arnold replied without hesitation. "Our team was playing a championship game, and the coach put me in like he always did when my father showed up for the game. It was the last inning with two outs, and the game was tied. There were two of my teammates on base, and all I had to do was hit a grounder, and we would have scored and won the game. I was so nervous when I came to bat that I peed in my pants. The pitcher threw the first two balls right down the middle, and I swung and missed at both. Then I heard the unmistakable voice of my father coming from the stands saying, "You don't hit this next pitch, Arnold, and you're gonna get it from me!" The pitch came, and I swung and missed. The people in the stands from the other team started screaming and hollering about winning the game. I stood there fearing the worst. When I turned to walk toward the dugout, I saw my father running toward me with the meanest face I'd ever seen him have. When he reached me, he hauled off, hit me in the face with his fist, and knocked me straight to the ground. The coach on our team came running over and pulled my dad away from me as he stood over me, screaming, "You are nothing but the scum of the earth!" *

"I'm so sorry to hear this, Arnold." Dr. Monroe lamented. "Did this type of behavior from your father only happen when you played sports?"

"Oh no," Arnold replied with his voice choking. "Though it was the first time he hit me. He would often belittle me in front of others over the smallest of things. Like one time, I left my bicycle out in the rain. The next day he took it away from me and ran over it with his car just to show me how mad he was at me for leaving it outside. I know kids need to be taught lessons, but isn't that a bit much?"

"Do you see yourself having children someday?" she asked.

"Well, I hope so," Arnold said, wondering what that had to do with his problem with his father.

"Have you ever heard the expression, 'the apple doesn't fall too far from the tree?' Dr. Monroe asked.

"Yeah, I think so," Arnold answered.

"With the abuse you've experienced from your father," Dr. Monroe continued, "you will need to be very aware of the apple and where you fall. We'll touch on this in future sessions."

"So, you think I could become an abusive person too?"

"Victims of abuse can repeat the behavior of their abuser. It is helpful to be aware of your own patterns of behavior as you navigate relationships, especially if you become a parent."

The ride back to Torrid Hills was filled with mixed emotions for Arnold, excited that tonight would be his first date with Sara, countered by the warning words of Dr. Monroe hanging over him like the ghostly dark clouds that filled the sky in the distance.

Could someday he be the apple from his father's tree?

*This story was told by a youth sports director at Ramstein Air Base

13

"Mom and Dad, this is Arnold," Sara said, tilting her head toward Arnold as if begging for their acceptance. "Arnold's dad is the person the park was named after the other day."

"Oh, nice to meet you." Jeff and Amanda said in unison. "I suppose you were quite proud to see your dad being honored that way." Amanda continued.

"Yes, it was nice." Was the extent of what Arnold could say as he forced back any hint of disagreement.

"We're going out for dinner," Sara said, glancing up and down at the clock as if they were late for a reservation.

"Well, we won't hold you up then. Have a great time." Jeff said while rushing them out the door.

Sara and Arnold talked about what all couples do on their first date, never getting around to the conversation they had at the Halloween event. It seemed too sensitive a subject for the occasion. After dinner, they decided to take a ride to "anywhere" as Arnold put it, seemingly, never wanting to end the night.

"How about we take a ride over to Greensboro," Arnold said. "I know a great bar with some great music."

"Sounds like a plan," Sara said, happy to let the night go on.

As they traveled to Greensboro, deep in conversation, a car sped past them when Arnold uttered, "I swear that was my father that just passed in that car. There was a woman with him. I think it was Linda Harris."

"Are you sure it was him?" Sara said. "And who is Linda Harris."

"She's the mayor's wife," Arnold said.

"Oh, maybe it's nothing. He could just be giving her a ride home." Sara said.

Arnold sped up to follow them. For the next few miles, Arnold's mind began to grow with anger. *"Is my father cheating on my mother? Was he always like this? If he is a cheater, maybe this is my way to get back at him for everything he has done to me."*

"You haven't said a word for the last ten minutes, Arnold," Sara told him. "I know it must be upsetting, but maybe we should just wait and see how this plays out before you get any more upset."

Entering Greensboro, Scotty's car turned into the *Greenwood Motel*. Arnold followed him there but kept his car at a distance.

Sara grabbed her cell phone and turned on her video, just in case. A few minutes later, Scotty came out of the motel office. When he got to his car, Linda jumped out as if the weight of the world was lifted from her shoulders. She grabbed Scotty and kissed him like they hadn't seen each other in weeks. They entered the motel room as Arnold sat there, confused like a mourner who had ventured into the wrong funeral parlor. But Sara, in all the excitement, had the wherewithal to capture it all on video.

There was a sense of paralysis overcoming Arnold as he sat stunned at what he had just witnessed. Sara, too, felt an emotional numbness overtaking her body when she finally said, "We need to get out of here, Arnold. We can't risk him seeing us."

"Some hero he turns out to be," Arnold growled, glancing around without really seeing anything. "You're right. Let's get out of here before I lose it."

What promised to be a great first date night turned into a heartbreaking night for Arnold. He wasn't about to dismiss what he had seen. "Not a chance," Arnold said to Sara as she urged him to try to forget it. "We need to follow up. I'm not letting him make a mockery of our family, no matter how much I resent everything he has done and said to me in the past."

"But we need to be careful," Sara suggested, feeling the sensation of things moving too quickly. "I know it looks awful, and you are hurt by what you just saw, but we need to make sure."

"What more do we have to see, Damnit!" Arnold blared out in anger. "You have it all on video." Sara sat, surprised that Arnold would react that way to her suggestion.

"All I'm saying, Arnold, is that we don't know one hundred percent what's happening in that room. Even though it seems obvious. We just need to act carefully."

"What do you suggest?" Arnold replied, calming down.

"I say that we make a plan for how we can follow up," Sara stated. "Let's go to that bar you suggested and get a drink. Maybe that will help settle us down for now and give us some ideas as to what to do."

"Why did it take me so long to meet someone like you?" Arnold said as he gazed lovingly at Sara.

Entering the *Hideaway Grill*, Arnold and Sara looked for an open table in a dark corner. A section where they could talk without being overheard.

"I think we should be careful," Sara began, "because your father is someone who, unfortunately, is respected in the community. No one would believe what we just saw. But the video doesn't lie and if we decide to confront him with it, I'm sure he will explode."

The two sat in conversation for a while. Then while paying the bill, the door opened. Scotty and Linda entered and sat down at the bar. Sara and Arnold tensed. Fortunately, the dark corner shielded them from being seen. They looked for a place for a quick exit, but there was none without walking past Scotty and Linda. Before long, Linda got up from the bar and headed to the restroom. Walking past Sara and Arnold, she glanced briefly through the dark toward them. They had their heads bowed, and Linda continued walking before turning around and looking once again at them.

"We've got to leave," Arnold said nervously. "I know she recognized me." With that, they both walked toward the door, looking away from Scotty. They opened the door and ran to the car. As they pulled away, Arnold hastily looked toward the lounge entrance. There stood Scotty looking at them as they sped off.

"He saw us." Sara cried out, her voice trembling.

"Yeah," said Arnold. "And the expression on his face told me that we could be in for trouble."

14

"Good morning, Sara," Emma said, bouncing on her toes and waving enthusiastically. "Come into my office. I've got some good news for you."

"Wow, now that's a great greeting first thing in the morning," Sara responded as if she owned the world. "So, what's the good news?"

"You know we have a Recreation Commission, right?" Emma said, trying to hold back a big smile.

"Sure, but what's that have to do with me?" Sara asked.

"Well, I received a text this morning saying that the Rec Commission wants to separate our department from them," Emma replied, still holding back her enthusiasm. "And if they do that, my responsibilities will be cut in half, but I still get the same pay."

"And again, you're telling me this because?" Sara asked.

"They have decided to name you the Recreation Director in charge of all the athletic programs in Torrid Hills," Emma yelled out to Sara with a huge grin.

"That's crazy!" Sara said, not believing what she had just heard. "I'm surprised that they picked me. I've only been here for a couple of months. Don't they usually do a recruitment search for a job this important?"

"Well, I guess you made a good impression on the commission's chairman," Emma said.

"And who would that be?" Sara asked.

"Linda Harris, the mayor's wife," Emma said. "Late last night, she called for an emergency meeting of the commission. She texted all the members and told them that she felt it was time that we named a person to run the recreation department and take the load off me so I can do my other duties. I'll be honest with you, the responsibility of overseeing the sports programs on the city fields is something I disliked more than anything, especially having to deal with parents and their attitudes."

Sara was stunned but managed to say, "So, you're telling me that if I accept the position, I'm getting into a can of worms, huh?"

Avoiding the question, Emma said, "I'm not sure the commission members were happy about being asked to make a decision that late at night. But when it's the mayor's wife, you don't have much of a choice."

As Emma talked, Sara sagged down in her chair with her head swiveling from side to side in disbelief. Did she hear Emma right? Did Linda call a special meeting late at night to make this decision? A smirk came to her face as she thought about Linda panicking after the *Hideaway Grill* fiasco. She needed to get out of there and contact Arnold as soon as possible.

"I'm overwhelmed," Sara said, wondering how this was all going to fold out.

"I forgot to mention," Emma said. "One thing that Linda said is that she would like to meet with you to discuss the agreement."

"Agreement?" Sara said, startled. "Why would I have to sign an agreement? If the Rec Commission is offering me the job, then that should be it. I should either accept or reject the offer."

"I agree," Emma replied. "It does seem strange that she would want you to sign an agreement. But I guess when you meet with her, you'll figure out why."

"Did she say when and where?" Sara asked.

"Yes, she asked if you could meet her at the park near the concession stand at 10:30 this morning."

"The park?" Sara said. "That's a strange place for someone to want to meet to sign an agreement. But, like you said, I guess I'll find out."

"I assume you'll accept the offer and take the position?" Emma asked with a quizzical look on her face. "You seem a little unsettled by all of this."

"Oh sure," Sara answered, looking far off in the distance. "I just want to take a few minutes to think things over. This all has happened so quickly."

"I understand," Emma said. "Why don't you take time off before your meeting and check back with me this afternoon? After all, this might be the last time I will be your boss. Linda Harris will be your boss in the future."

Hearing that Linda Harris would be her boss was a gut punch to Sara. It's one thing to meet face to face with the woman she just recorded at a motel room with Arnold's father. But how awkward it would be to have her as a boss. But then, she thought cynically... *perhaps I will always have the upper hand.* With that, she picked up her cell phone and texted Arnold, "Emergency, *meet me at Andy's ASAP!*"

"Be there in 15 minutes. I have something to tell you too." Arnold's return text said.

Sara arrived at *Andy's* first and grabbed a table in the corner. She couldn't sit still, fidgeting and biting her nails. She was so anxious she had to run to the restroom.

"If Arnold comes in, tell him I'm at the table over in the corner." She said hastily to Andy.

"Sure will. It's nice to see you, Sara." Andy said in a snappish way.

"Oh, sorry, Andy." She said, rushing to the restroom. "It's good to see your too."

It was no sooner than ten seconds when Arnold walked in the door.

"She's here.." Andy yelled to Arnold. "She got the table over there in the corner before she went to the restroom."

"Thanks, Andy," Arnold replied, looking nervously at the table. "Must be early for customers since we're the only ones here."

He sat down, and a moment later, Sara came out and almost sprinted to the table.

"This has been the craziest twenty-four hours I can ever remember," Sara told Arnold, trying to catch her breath. "You're not going to believe this. I've been offered the job as the Director of Recreation for the City of Torrid Hills."

"What?" Arnold yelled, causing Andy to look over quizzically.

Sara lowered her voice almost to a whisper and said, "You're not going to believe this but guess who decided late last night to convince the Rec Commission to hire me?"

"Okay, who?" Arnold said, looking at Sara like a dog, anxious to take a walk.

"Linda Harris." She declared, grinning from ear to ear.

"You're shitting me." Arnold gasped. "This is getting wilder by the minute. Are you ready to hear what my news is?"

"I can't believe it would be any weirder than what I just told you."

"Oh yeah?" Arnold bolted back. "What would you say if I told you that my father just offered to give me the cottage he has down by the lake."

"Oh, my lord." Sara sat motionless. "We have them both backed in a corner, and they think the only way out is to give us something to keep us quiet."

"So, what do we do now," Arnold asked.

"Well, I have a meeting with Linda at 10:30 to sign some kind of agreement," Sara responded. "We'll see how that goes. What about you?"

"My father wants to meet with me to discuss the cottage this afternoon," Arnold said. "I guess we could get together tonight to celebrate our newfound future or cry in our beer."

"So, back to the *Hideaway* in Greensboro?" Sara asked Arnold.

"Works for me," Arnold replied. "I'll pick you up at 6:30."

"Are you sure we're both not having the same weird dream?" Arnold asked. He was feeling wary and excited at the same time.

"Or maybe nightmare," Sara answered.

15

On the drive to the park, Sara felt a knot in her stomach. She was about to meet the woman, who just a few hours earlier, she had videoed coming out of a motel room with Arnold's father. As she exited the car and walked toward the empty ball fields, she felt like she was standing on the edge of a frozen pond, forced to go forward, not knowing how thick the ice was. Standing next to the concession stand was Linda Harris, with a folder in her hand. Sara's knees buckled as she walked toward her before saying, "Good morning, nice to see you."

"I have another meeting Sara, so maybe we can make this quick," Linda suggested abruptly.

"Okay," Sara responded. "Emma told me earlier this morning that you have selected me to be the Recreation Department Director."

"That's true," Linda replied, seeming on edge.

Like the elephant in the room scenario, neither Linda nor Sara wanted to look each other in the eye, fearing last night's memory might set off a firestorm.

"Here is the agreement I have created for you to review," Linda said as she handed the one sheet of paper to Sara.

Looking over the agreement, Sara said, "Well, this seems simple enough. Unless I'm mistaken, it says that I agree to the stated salary and will perform my duties as the Director of Recreation to the best of my abilities. Right?"

"That's correct," Linda responded. "Except for the one last sentence."

"Oh, sorry, I missed that part," Sara said. "It says,

Additional stipulation; In the event the Director of Recreation should say anything insinuating or derogatory about any member of the Recreation Commission, then said Director can be fired immediately."

"Well, that seems strange," Sara said, knowing full well what Linda had in mind. "But I have no trouble signing the agreement."

"Well, that's great. The job is yours for as long as you want it." Linda replied, looking relieved. "Sorry, I have to get to another meeting. Nice meeting you, Sara. Good luck."

Watching Linda drive away, Sara stood with her mouth agape feeling mentally numb and unable to focus. Despite everything that had happened in the last twenty-four hours, she now had a new future. She, in fact, was the Director of Recreation. How good did that sound? And she could keep the job for as long as she wanted unless, of course, she decided to spill the beans on the Linda/Scotty affair.

Before getting into her car and driving back to the office, Sara picked up her phone and called Arnold.

"Well, it's now official," Sara said with a grin that couldn't be contained. "You are now talking to the official Director of Recreation for the city of Torrid Hills, North Carolina."

"Holy shit!" Arnold exclaimed. "That was quick. What did she say? Any mention at all about last night?"

"She couldn't get out of there quick enough," Sara said. "Basically, I can keep the job as long as I want, as long as I don't say anything bad about her."

"Unbelievable," Arnold replied.

"Well, the contract actually said *any* of the board members, so it wouldn't sound suspicious, but we know what it meant," Sara said with a smirk.

"Now, I've got to see what happens with my dad this afternoon," Arnold said with hope in his voice.

"Well, I hope it goes as well as mine went," Sara responded.

"We'll see," Turning to get in his car. "I'm meeting him at 2:00 at the cottage. Let's hope I end up with a deal as good as you got."

As Arnold drove back to the hotel, he received a text from an unknown number. "Meet me at your dad's cottage at 1PM. Your dad had an emergency meeting he had to go to."

It was close to 1PM at the time, so Arnold decided to drive to the cottage and meet with the person who texted him.

Scotty's cottage was located about four miles from Torrid Hills. It sat on a lake overlooking the Blue Ridge mountains. The beautiful site was filled with trees surrounding the shoreline like a stadium for Saturday afternoon football. Arnold envisioned the day he and Sara could someday be living there. How serendipitous it was that he and Sara had caught his dad and the mayor's wife at the motel, and now his dad was offering him his own cottage. *Time heals all wounds*, Arnold thought.

As he pulled into the lane toward the cottage, up ahead, he saw a car sitting out front. The thought that perhaps the strange text he had received was from a bank employee crossed his mind. 'Maybe he's here to have me sign the deed,' he thought. As he stepped from his car, a burly, tough-looking man in his mid-thirties walked toward him. Arnold hesitated. 'This guy is not a banker,' he thought.

"Scotty told me to leave you with a message." The stranger said, causing the hair on Arnold's arms and neck to rise. His legs began to wobble, sensing ultimate doom.

"You mention anything about what you might have seen in Greensboro last night to anyone, and this gun will find you. You get it?" The man yelled in Arnold's face.

With beads of sweat dripping from his forehead, Arnold replied, "Yes, sir."

Tapping the stock of his gun on Arnold's shoulder, Scotty's obvious messenger added. "I sure hope I don't have to use this thing because I hate wasting bullets. Have a nice day." As he drove off, Arnold took out his cell phone and quickly took a photo of the man's license plate, hoping he didn't see him in his rearview mirror.

Shaken by the whole experience, Arnold stood there for a long time before getting in his car. Fifteen minutes before, he had envisioned a world where he and Sara would spend time together at this beautiful cottage on the lake. But once again his father had shattered his hopes with threats to have him killed. Would it ever end? Would he ever entirely escape the abusiveness his father had inflicted on him since the day he was born? Not wanting to bring Sara into his world of invectiveness, he decided to tell her he could no longer see her.

16

"I'd rather not talk about it," Arnold said to Sara over the phone. "I think it might be best if we stopped seeing each other."

"Wait, what are you talking about?" Sara responded with alarm. "The last time we talked, you were all excited about your father giving you the cottage by the lake. Now, you don't even want to talk to me. What happened? Why do you not want us to keep seeing each other?"

"I don't deserve someone like you, Sara." Arnold cried out. "My family is untrustworthy, and I don't want you to be part of something so undermining."

"Can you at least tell me what happened at the meeting with your father?" Sara asked, hoping Arnold would respond.

"I can't," Arnold said emphatically.

"You can't?" Sara yelled. "What does that mean?"

"I said I can't talk about it!" Arnold replied as he hung up the phone.

Sara stood for what seemed an eternity, baffled by the conversation with Arnold. Her phone vibrated, and she jumped. It was Cathy.

"Hey, just calling to catch up. How'd your date with Arnold go?"

"He just told me he doesn't want to see me again. He's acting crazy. He even hung up on me! I'm really worried about him."

"Wow, that's crazy," Cathy said. "You want me to try and talk to him to see what's going on? Maybe I can get to the bottom of it."

"No, that's okay. I'll work it out with him, hopefully." Sara replied.

"Shouldn't you get to work before you get fired?" Cathy said. "It's almost 9:00."

"Oh, that's not gonna happen," Sara said. "I just got promoted to be the Director of Recreation."

"What? You're kidding me?" Cathy said. "How in the hell did you get that job? You've only been there a couple months!"

"It seems strange, I know," Sara replied hesitantly, not wanting to give away any hint of wrongdoing. "The mayor's wife Linda Harris, who is the Chairman of the Rec Commission, told Emma that she thought I should be the director."

"Wait. You mean, right out of the blue, the mayor's wife wants to name you the director without any interview or anything?"

"Yep," Sara answered quickly, hoping Cathy would change the subject.

"That just doesn't add up, Sara," Cathy said impatiently. "Sounds like you're not telling me the whole story."

"Hey, sorry, but I gotta run." Sara replied anxiously, "I'll talk to you soon. Love you!"

Rushing into the office, Sara was greeted by Emma and her staff with a huge banner saying, "CONGRATULATIONS to the new Director of Recreation, Sara Tobin."

Sara was overwhelmed. "Thank you, guys!" she said with a huge smile.

"I wish you well in your new job Sara," Emma said, sounding congratulatory. "Just don't let the pressures of the 'win at all costs' parent atmosphere get to you."

"Don't worry, Emma," Sara replied. "I'm sure there will be a lot of people that will want to run me out of town when I set the new rules. But there will be changes for all the leagues who use our facilities. I've seen enough abuse so far to make some people's blood curdle."

Just then, Sara's phone buzzed. Cathy was calling again.

"Hey, I just ran into Arnold," Cathy said. "He told me he couldn't talk about why he didn't want to see you anymore. I don't know what's going on, Sara, but I've known you long enough to say that something doesn't seem right. And it's not something between the two of you. It's something else. What is it?" Cathy said, annoyed that Sara and Arnold were obviously keeping a secret. "I thought we were friends. Why won't you tell me what's going on with you?"

Sara thought for a minute.

"If you can convince Arnold to meet with us, I'll tell you what it's all about," Sara answered, never wanting to lose her friendship with Cathy.

"I'll call you back," Cathy said with a voice, rushing as if she had left the cake burning in the oven.

17

The first day on the job was exciting for Sara. But one thing was certain. She needed an assistant. The town of Torrid Hills provided far and few candidates qualified for the job. So, she went out on a limb and asked Cathy if she might be interested.

"Not a chance," Cathy replied. "I had my fill of that whole nonsense."

"Why do you say that? You sound like the perfect person I'm looking for." Sara exclaimed. "I'm looking for someone who understands what goes on with kids playing sports. Something has to change."

"You really want to know?" Cathy exclaimed, with anger spreading through her like a malignant tumor. "When I was fourteen, my little brother Jimmy played little league baseball. He was ten years old and small for his age. The problem with that age group is some kids are early maturers and big for their age. It's a big problem with organized sports. With late-maturing little kids playing alongside and against kids that look more like teenagers than 10-year-olds. It's a joke and it's dangerous."

"I agree," Sara replied.

"One day," Cathy continued, "his team was playing the league's leading team. They had a couple of those bigger kids on their team. One of the boys, I swear, was five feet six and towered over the other kids. You ever watch the Little League World Series on TV? If you have, the first thing you notice is that there are a bunch of kids that look way older than what they are."

"Yeah, I've noticed they seem big for their age," Sara said.

"Well, in the game my brother was playing, the pitcher on the other team looked twice the size of Jimmy but was 10 years old too. Every time he threw the ball, the people on the other team let out a scream that sounded like they were in Yankee Stadium. The ball flew by Jimmy at an unbelievable speed. I could see him shaking. He was so nervous. I hid my hands over my face cause I was so scared he would get hurt. Then I looked just in time to see Jimmy raise the bat over his head. The pitch came flying by and landed squarely on Jimmy's ribcage. He dropped to the ground. Everyone started screaming."

"Oh my god!" Sara exclaimed.

"Jimmy lay there motionless. People crammed around, not knowing what to do. My dad and mom were trying to do anything they could to revive him. Finally, the ambulance arrived, but within a few minutes of working on him, they declared Jimmy dead."

"That is so tragic and unfair losing your little brother that way." Sara lamented.

"The same unfair thing happens in all kids' sports," Cathy added. "Think of what happens in football. The coach picks the early maturing kid to be the quarterback or running back. They run all over the smaller kids. It's all a joke, but like I said a dangerous joke."

"Some people say you can be part of the problem, or you can be part of the solution," Sara stated to Cathy with a pleading sound. "I'm giving you a chance to be part of the solution. I really want to make changes, especially because of the terrible things that can happen to kids like your brother."

"Let me think about it, Sara," Cathy said.

"That's all I can ask. I'm glad you told me about your brother. I'm sure your family has never gotten over that." Sara said.

"It's been tough for my parents. But they may be happy to hear that I could be part of the solution to make it better." Cathy mused.

"Well, keep this in mind," Sara responded. "It won't be an easy task. Most of these parents and coaches cannot see the forest for the trees out there. They will find an argument for every sensible change we want to make. The important thing is that I've got the backing of Linda Harris whether she likes where I'm going or not."

"Are you ever going to tell me what that is all about?" Cathy replied.

Sara decided to fill Cathy in on everything. She needed someone to talk to about it, and with Arnold avoiding her, who better than her new best friend.

All the gory details cascaded from Sara's mouth like the waterfall at Lakewood Mountain.

"Holy shit, Sara! That's a lot to take in!" Cathy exclaimed. "So, I'm guessing she panicked and gave you the job hoping to keep you quiet."

"Yeah, you're probably right. But what about being my assistant? I know it's a lot." Sara replied. "Do you think you still might be interested?"

"Like I said, let me think about it. But I do like challenges." Cathy said with a smile. "In the meantime, we need to figure out how to get Arnold to come to his senses. It had to be something weird that happened between him and his father. I'll find out."

18

The vision of his father's hired goon pointing a gun at him had made Arnold paranoid. Walls seemed to be crashing around him like bricks from a falling building. The future he had hoped to build with the girl of his dreams now seemed bleak. The never-ending abuses he faced as a child filled Arnold with the desire to end it all. Feeling depressed and desperate, he somehow had the presence of mind to call Dr. Monroe's office. Perhaps she could help him with the pain and suffering he was experiencing.

"Hello, is Dr. Monroe available for any appointments today?" Arnold said to the receptionist, with despair in his voice.

"She is, but she's only taking emergency appointments today. Is your case an emergency?" The receptionist replied.

"Yes, I really need to meet with her. Please tell her it is Arnold Jones from Torrid Hills." Arnold responded bleakly.

"Hold for a minute." replied the receptionist. Then after a brief hold said, "Can you come in at 2PM?"

"Yes, I'll be there," Arnold answered, feeling relief.

On his way to Greensboro, Arnold's mind was swirling with foreboding thoughts of how he had no will to live. What did he do to deserve the constant darkening and disheartening voice of his father? It was too much to bear, and it made him feel worthless. 'Why should he go on living?' captivated his mind. The mental pain was excruciating.

When he reached Dr. Monroe's office, he forced himself to get out of the car. The mental pain between his eyes seemed to be twirling like a pinwheel.

"Dr. Monroe will see you now." the receptionist said.

As he entered the room, a flash of pain went through Arnold like the ripple of sheet lightning.

Dr. Monroe looked at Arnold and, seeing his expression, said, "I think you should sit down."

Arnold sat motionless for what seemed an eternity before he was able to cry out, "I need help!"

For the next forty-five minutes, Arnold told the psychologist of all the trauma he had faced in the past few days. With her help, he realized he needed someone like Sara in his life to help him get through times like these. He didn't need to push her away. He needed to push his father away. He and Sara didn't have to go anywhere near his awful family. Maybe his life would change for the better with her by his side.

Arnold thanked Dr. Monroe and headed back to Torrid Hills, feeling much better than when he walked into her office. On the drive, he decided to call Sara.

"I am so sorry for how I've been behaving, Sara," he said, thinking of the day he laid eyes on her for the first time. "Can we meet maybe at the park to talk?"

"Sure," Sara said with tears welling up in her eyes. "I'll meet you there in twenty minutes."

Arnold suddenly felt an unexpected release of tension come over his body. Dr. Monroe was right. All he needed was the comforting sound of a voice he trusted. His depression seemed to disappear like a dark cloud running from the sun.

Two hours passed before Sara and Arnold happily reached a cathartic moment when they vowed to continue their relationship. Andy's Grill became their favorite spot to meet with friends like Cathy, who herself had met what she called "The love of her life."

Over the next several months, Sara's job became more challenging than she thought it would be. Fortunately, she had the video of Linda and Scotty tucked away in case of need. Arnold was promoted to manager at the Torrid Hills Inn. He stayed a far distance from his father. He hadn't spoken to him after what happened at the cabin.

It wouldn't be long before Sara and Arnold announced they would be having a child, a boy. And they would be calling him Billy.

19

It was an early nostalgic Fall in Torrid Hills, North Carolina, with the colors of the red maples, hickory and sweet gum leaves trickling down like spinning color wheels amongst the nearby forest. In her ninth month of pregnancy, Sara Jones struggled, step by step, as she waddled across the kitchen floor, desperate to reach the closest chair. The constant movement inside her belly gave the feeling of an oversized load of laundry tumbling its way to dryness on this crisp autumn day.

It seemed like yesterday to Sara and Arnold when Billy was inside her belly, wanting to get out. Yet it was five years ago. She had asked her friend Cathy to marry her and Arnold in a quiet ceremony. To make it legal, Cathy agreed to apply for her Notary Public. On the day of the "ceremony," she stood stoically, unsmiling like a full-fledged religious figure, even though, according to her, she hadn't been in a church for the last twenty-five years. Thus, the married life of Sara and Arnold Jones began.

A few months later, unexpected as a February heat wave in North Carolina, Sara announced to Arnold that they were having a baby. Filled with joy, they decided his name would be Billy.

Billy learned to crawl early, walk early, and just about everything early, causing Arnold to say, "Looks like we might have a champion athlete here."

Now at 5 years old, Billy was always anxious to get outside and play with friends. He asked Sara if he could meet with his friend Ryan and play on the playground.

"All right, Billy," Sara said, looking across the street to the park. Beyond the swings and sliding boards were the ballfields where she had overseen the sports programs for the past five years. "Be sure that you two don't wander off somewhere where I can't look out the window and see you."

As Director of Recreation, Sara's responsibility was overseeing parent groups that ran the football, soccer, and baseball programs. They were required to apply for and receive permits from the city to use the fields during their respective seasons.

It hadn't been a fun time for Sara dealing with the parent groups in Torrid Hills. It all began when Phil Albertson and Thelma Fihurty, who both went to Torrid Hills High School became close friends. They were so close that not long after high school, they decided to spend weekends together, even though both were married to other people. While sneaking off to motels outside of town, they ran up sizeable bills, which they soon couldn't pay. One motel owner, Roland Powenner, who went to high school with both of them, promised to divulge their rendezvous with the public if they didn't settle the money they owed. Scared out of his wits, Phil, who was president of the Torrid Hill Little League, decided to name Thelma as the head of the concession stands. Many evenings during games, the concession stands would bring in a few hundred dollars. Since there was no one to oversee the amount profited, Phil and Thelma decided it would be an easy way to skim money and soon have enough to pay off their hotel debt. It was easy for a while, but when it came time to pay for the umpires, Alfred Ragman, the head of the umpire's association, was told by Thelma that they would have to wait for a couple weeks before being paid. Alfred didn't take the news well, and since he was aware that the funds to pay the umpires came from the concession stand profits, he asked for an audit of the concession stand. That wasn't good news for Phil and Thelma. It didn't take long before the little league board discovered that, sure enough, Thelma was the guilty one, skimming hundreds of dollars. Thelma got pissed when they didn't arrest Phil, too, because, as she told Jack Aliman, the city solicitor, "It was Phil's idea all along. Why should I be the only one guilty?" Unlucky for Phil, after he and Thelma paid off the umpires and the Little League organization, he got fired from his job at the local Stop and Go. Thelma ended up going on social security. Both had to pay a fine of $1000 and do serve community service for a year. Roland Powenner, the motel owner, sued both of them for what they owed him. *

Looking out the window to check on Billy, Sara spotted Cathy's car pulling up to the house. As she watched Cathy walk toward the house, she couldn't help but think how lucky she was to have convinced Cathy to be her assistant. She was there at every moment to back Sara up on issues with the leagues. On the other hand, Sara was there to back Cathy in her love life.

Cathy had become the jealous type after two previous marriage failures. Once again, her jealousy let her emotions get in the way. She and Ian Deladonte, a truck driver for the Torrid Hills's Tobacco Plant, had been dating for the past three years and talked of marriage. One evening, when waiting in line at McDonald's, she spotted Ian two cars ahead with a woman sitting next to him. In a rage, filled with adrenaline rushing through her body like piping hot water from a kitchen faucet, she jumped from her car and ran to Ian's car, screaming, "YOU CHEATER!" As she looked in the window, a shaken Ian said, "Uh, hi Cathy, meet my sister, Barbara." Cathy froze in space. Stuttering and stammering and growing more frustrated, the words refused to come out. Waves of shame ran through her like savage internal blushes before she could force out a "sorry."

It was three weeks before Cathy was able to climb out of her shell of shame and call Ian. She hadn't heard from him in all that time and felt terrible that she had embarrassed him in front of his sister. With her voice trembling and hands shaking, she dialed his number. "Hello," came the voice of a woman. "Ian isn't in now. Can I help you?". With that, Cathy hung up the phone. Surely, Ian's sister wouldn't still be there after all this time. So, Cathy decided to contact a private investigator, Maurice Tambly. He was known to be the most successful PI in North Carolina.

It didn't take long before Maurice called Cathy with the answer. It appears Mr. Deladonte didn't have a sister. His research found that Ian had at least 2 other fiancés in the state of North Carolina. Anger welled up in Cathy like lava in a volcano. Ian had led her on for the past three years, even proposing to her. In her rage, Cathy decided to get even. She filled a large bucket with sand and poured the contents down the gas tank in Ian's brand-new Truck. Revenge was like biting the dog that bit you. Ian got the message, though he couldn't confirm it was Cathy who did the dastardly deed.

"Oh, you are the vengeful one, Miss Cathy," Sara said with a smirk on her face.

"But it feels soooo good," Cathy replied. "The bastard deserved it!"

Looking out the window, Sara looked for Billy. Not seeing him, she went to the front door and yelled his name. "BILLY!", TIME TO COME IN." A knot crept up her stomach to her throat when there was no response from Billy. She and Cathy ran to the park, looking all around with no sight of him. Sara clutched at her heart as if tigers were tearing it apart. "Where is Ryan?" she screamed to no one. They were both on the sliding board the last time she looked, when Cathy was walking up her driveway. It was only a few moments ago.

* Based on a true story. Authorities charge that more than $1.4 million in one state was stolen from youth sports leagues over a 10-year period.

20

Filled with terror and a heartbeat thrashing in her ears, Sara scoured the playground hoping for anything that would provide a positive outcome. She yelled "BIIIILLY!" again and again.

Hearing her screams, Ryan's mother came out of her house and raced toward Sara. "Ryan said that a man came up to him and Billy and wanted to show Billy the ballfield!" She said with fear in her voice.

"What ballfield, WHAT BALLFIELD?' Sara screamed.

"He didn't say." Ryan's mother replied.

Breathing heavily, Cathy yelled out to Sara, "The closest one is the little league field over next to Walnut Street. Let's run over there."

The two took off running toward the little league field, and as they got close, they saw a man sitting in the dugout with Billy. As they got closer, they saw it was Scotty Jones. Anger and rage whistled through Sara like the night wind on a desert. She ran into the dugout and grabbed Billy while repulsively screaming at Scotty, "HOW COULD YOU DO THIS, YOU IDIOT?"

"Don't be so upset, missy," Scotty said. "You seem to forget that this young man is my grandson. I was just taking him here to show him what a ballfield looks like. Something I'm sure his father would never think of doing. And while I'm at it, you seem to also forget whose name is on the sign as you enter this park."

Sara struggled to contain herself. With Cathy at her side, she looked at Scotty and, with a slow and steady breath, said, "You'll pay for this." Then stormed out of the dugout toward home.

As the three walked back toward Sara's house, Sara stopped and said, "Billy, I'm so sorry that I had to yell at your grandfather, but he should have told me he was taking you to the field. You know how worried I was about you, right?" Sara said, placing her arms around Billy and hugging him tightly.

"I know, Mommy. I'm sorry." Billy said. "Grandpa just told me that he wanted me to see where he was going to help me become a great ballplayer like he was. He said he's going to be my coach."

"No, he isn't Billy," Sara replied. "Your dad is going to be your coach."

With that, Cathy looked at Sara as if she had been hit by a blast from a giant hair dryer.

"That's right," Cathy said, looking at Sara questionably. "He'll be the best coach in the league!"

"What are you going to tell Arnold?" Cathy asked as she and Sara reached the front door, and Billy ran inside.

"I'm not sure," Sara answered Cathy, wanting to avoid the question. "But I'll tell you one thing; that man will never spend more than two minutes with Billy in the future.

"I'm surprised Billy even knows his grandfather with the relationship you and Arnold have with him," Cathy responded.

"He and Martha started dropping by unannounced when Billy was about 2 years old," Sara replied. "They show up with presents and act like they are the sweetest people around, but they barely acknowledge Arnold and me. I swear that woman hasn't said ten words to me in all the time I've known her."

When Arnold walked in the door that night, Billy ran up to him as if Arnold had an armful of Christmas presents and said, "Dad! You're gonna be my baseball coach!"

"Uh, ok," Arnold said, looking out of the corner of his eye toward Sara. "How about your mom and I talk about it while you go up to your room and play for a while."

"You're not going to like what I have to tell you, so brace yourself," Sara said to Arnold as they sat at the kitchen table.

Hearing the complete story, Arnold, filled with anger, like a wounded bull in a ring, exclaimed, "That good for nothing, son of a bitch! He's now trying to come between my son and me?"

"The best way to get back at him, Arnold, is to go out there and be Billy's coach. Show him you are not letting him get away with it." Sara told Arnold.

"When does T-ball start?" Arnold asked.

"Sign-ups start next week, and the season begins the first of April," Sara replied with a glint of hope in her eyes.

"I'm getting him all he needs to start practicing in the backyard," Arnold said with a sense of a man on a mission.

21

Springtime in Torrid Hills felt like new fresh sheets. Daffodils, tulips, and pansies lined the sidewalks. People breathed in the air like it flowed from a gigantic oxygen mask. And it was time for T-ball.

"C'mon, Dad." Billy would yell at Arnold while nearly pulling him out of bed. Arnold had promised to start each morning practicing baseball with Billy before school. "I'm gonna be the best player in T-ball! That's what my grandpa says." The words bit Arnold like a crazed and starving wolf.

"Be patient with him out there," Sara warned as he and Billy went out to the backyard. "He's just five years old and may not have tracking skills yet."

"What are tracking skills?" Arnold said with a puzzled look as if Sara was a scientist teaching aerodynamics.

"It's like hand and eye coordination," Sara replied. "Some kids have no problem watching and catching a ball. Others get scared when one is thrown at them. You'll find out soon enough. Just make it fun for him."

Arnold walked out back and tossed the ball to Billy. "Okay, let's get this thing going, Mr. T-Ball player."

"Wow, that was great, Billy!" Arnold exclaimed as Billy caught ball after ball with ease. "Time to get ready for school." Arnold puffed his chest out, feeling he had a true athlete about to emerge from the Arnold Jones household.

"You wouldn't believe it, Sara!" Arnold cried out. "He's a natural! I can't wait until the season starts, and I sure can't wait to see the look on my father's face when he sees the next Jones family top athlete."

"Don't get your hopes up too soon," Sara responded with a warning tone. "You know firsthand how bad things can get when pressure is put on a kid."

The following Saturday, Arnold and Billy jumped in the car and headed down to the Brad Picket Sporting Goods Store to buy a T-ball set.

"Just two more weeks, Billy, before sign-ups and tryouts," Arnold said as they traveled down Torrid Avenue. Filled with pride, like a father whose kid had won every event at that year's field day, Arnold said, "You getting excited, Billy?"

"What's tryouts, Dad?" Billy asked as if it were some other game he had to learn how to play.

"Well, all the kids that want to play T-ball this year go to the park, then all the dads who are coaches pick the players they want on their team."

"Will you pick me to be on your team?" Billy said with a worried look on his face.

"I haven't signed up to coach, so we'll see what happens," Arnold said.

It looked like Arnold wasn't the only father in town who was teaching their kid to get ready for T-Ball. Brad's store was filled with dads looking for any kind of baseball equipment to get their kids ready. Fortunately for Arnold and Billy, they were able to buy a T-ball set before they ran out. They headed for home, anxious to get out in the backyard and start swinging the bat.

Running into the house all frenzied, Billy ran to his room to change for practice.

"I don't want to upset you, Arnold," Sara said. "Cathy just called me and said that your dad has been elected president of the Torrid Hills Youth League Baseball Association. And it means he will oversee all the different divisions …including T-Ball."

"Oh shit," Arnold exclaimed. "But wait, aren't you technically over him? You're the Recreation Director."

Sara's mouth curled like a half-moon smile as she calmly replied, "And if he gets in our way, don't forget, I still have a video that he would never want anyone to see."

With bitterness as a mourning day, Arnold leaned toward her and said, "I will never forget that."

Trying not to let the news about his father bother him too much, Arnold yelled upstairs, "Let's get out there and try the new T-Ball stand, Billy."

"Okay, Dad, I gotta put my baseball shirt on first." An excited Billy said.

As they walked out to the backyard to practice, it wasn't two minutes later before Ryan's mother, Margaret Signote knocked on the front door.

"Have you got a minute, Sara?" She said, looking out the back door as Arnold and Billy began practicing with their new T-Ball set.

"What's up?" Sara said.

"Earlier today, Billy told Ryan he was signing up for T-Ball this year," Margaret said. "Peter doesn't want Ryan to play T-Ball. As you know, he's a musician, and he wants Ryan to focus on learning the piano. Can you ask Arnold if he would talk to Peter and try to convince him to let Ryan play T-Ball?"

"I really feel for you, Margaret," Sara replied, wanting to say anything that might help. "But don't you think both you and Peter should ask Ryan what he wants to do? I mean, it's his life, and taking away something he might really enjoy just doesn't seem fair."

"I knew you'd say something like that," Margaret said, looking disappointed. "It's just Peter doesn't even give Ryan a chance to try. And I feel so guilty that he sees Billy having so much fun."

"Well, who knows, Margaret, Ryan may enjoy music," Sara said, trying to soothe her.

"I know," Margaret said, walking out the door. "But Peter is just so demanding when it comes to Ryan taking piano lessons."

"I feel for you, Margaret." Sara offered. "I hope it all works out. I'll mention it to Arnold. Maybe he can give Peter a little push toward T-ball."

22

"Cathy, pack your bags!" Sara yelled from her office.

"What, am I being fired?" Cathy replied.

"Not yet," Sara said. "We're going to Memphis."

"You're kidding, right?" Cathy said, eager as a sprinter at the starting gate.

"I just got an invitation to a national youth sports conference in Memphis. Everything on the agenda covers things we need to find out about for our program." Sara said, sounding as eager as Cathy.

"When do we leave?" Cathy said. "And who's going to pay for it?"

"Well, that shouldn't be a problem. I'll just call my good friend Linda Harris and tell her we need to go." Sara said.

"You're milking the Linda bit for all you can get, girl," Cathy said. "Who do you think will be at the conference?"

"The invite said recreation directors who are responsible for youth sports in their communities are invited and that our assistants were welcome too. There will be rec directors from all over the country." Sara answered.

"Sounds exciting," Cathy said. "Maybe we can learn how to handle some of those idiots we'll have to deal with once the season gets going."

"Yeah, I like the idea of hearing what experts have to say about dealing with *those* types of parents and coaches." Sara offered. "And we can take a course to become certified as a Youth Sports Administrator."

"Youth Sports Administrator," Cathy repeated. "Damn, I could sound like someone important!" she said with a cheeky grin.

It wasn't long before Sara and Cathy landed in Memphis. On the first day of the conference, Cathy caught a handsome man eyeing her up. Eric Gallant walked up to Cathy and said, "I saw you yesterday when you were registering at the hotel. I bet you can't wait til tomorrow." To which Cathy asked, "Why?"

Eric replied, "Because you get better looking every day."

That was it. One thing Cathy liked in the opposite sex was a sense of humor.

"Wow, that's a good one," Cathy said with a chuckle. Eager to continue the conversation, she asked, "So, where are you from?"

"I'm from the big metropolis of Platsburg, North Carolina," Eric replied. "Ever hear of it?"

"Hear of it? Are you kidding? I live about twenty miles from there." Cathy continued, feeling like she just might have landed the biggest fish in the lakes of North Carolina.

"Really?" Eric said as he began to feel like he held a hand full of aces in a poker game. "So, you got any plans for after today's session?"

"No," Cathy responded with a smirk on her face. "I usually have three or four guys hitting me up, but I guess you got here first. What do you have in mind?"

"I found a great bar called *Rambo Rocks* a couple blocks from my hotel. It's got great vibes. Wanna go? We can talk about youth sports and stuff."

"What stuff?" Cathy asked, wanting to put Eric on the spot with her own type of humor.

"Oh, you know, just stuff," Eric replied, feeling he had met his match.

"Okay, maybe after my last session today. It's called *"How to Deal with Guys Who Try to Hit on You."* You want to meet me after the session?"

"Gee, I never saw that topic listed in the program." Eric muttered under his breath, "But I'll do one better. I'll sit next to you at the session."

"Okay," Cathy said with a shy giggle. "It's actually called *The Vicarious parent- Looking at their Kids like it was them out there."*

"Sounds like my league parents," Eric said. "I'll meet you there."

Talking outside after the session, Eric commented to Cathy, "Man, that made a lot of sense. So many parents think it's them out there on the field as they watch their kids play. The worst kind are the ones who never excelled on the field or court. They sit there cringing, wanting to make sure their kid doesn't screw up. And when their kid does, it's like they have a mental breakdown. They remember themselves screwing up, and it infuriates them to the point that they start screaming and yelling at anyone in sight. They just completely lose it. I remember one parent coming up to his kid after he lost a swimming meet by, I swear, one foot. He leans over the edge of the pool where his son is resting and says, "You are the scum of the earth. You let that other kid beat you." *

"Oh my god Eric." Cathy cried out. "You need to meet Sara, my boss. She is dealing with the same thing with her husband. He had an abusive father like that. And now that man just became the president of the little league organization where her kid is going to be playing Tee Ball."

"That sounds like a good conversation for us to have at Rambo's," Eric said, looking at Cathy pleadingly. "It's a short walk from here."

"You ever hear the word serendipitous, Eric?" Cathy asked half seriously as they walked toward the bar.

"Of course," Eric replied, pretending he had been insulted. "I did go to college. I even graduated Cuma Suma Laude."

"You're kidding?" Cathy responded.

"Yep, I'm kidding. I hardly got through. As a matter of fact, you're the first person I've told this to; I cheated on my last exam."

"I knew there was something sinister about you," Cathy said, holding back a chuckle.

"Coming in?" Eric asked Cathy as he held the door for her at *Rambo Rocks.*

"What and miss out on hearing all about your life story, Mr. Suma Cum Laude. I wouldn't miss it for the world."

At no time in her young life had Cathy ever met someone who floored her with such charm and humor. The minutes turned into hours as they talked about everything from riding a bicycle as a child to vacation times with their parents. It was midnight when they left the bar. Eric said, "How about coming over to my room for a nightcap."

"Where the hell were you last night, young lady?" Sara barked at Cathy. Sounding like an overbearing mother.

"I met this guy after my first session yesterday, and guess what! He's from Platsburg. It's only 20 miles from Torrid Hills." Cathy said, looking a little sheepish.

"And your point is?" Sara said.

"Well, he did know a lot about youth sports, and we got so deep in conversations that it was almost midnight, and then I forgot our room number and…."

"Just stop!" Sara said. "We came here to learn from the experts. Save your playtime for when we get home. There's a session today called *How to Deal with the Obnoxious Parents.*" I think we should both attend. Just last week, some woman named Andrea Stand came into my office bitching and complaining about the way we organize the schedules for the teams using the fields."

"Sorry about last night," Cathy said, not sounding entirely truthful in her demeanor.

"Yeah, yeah, yeah…" Sara responded with the seriousness of a mother scolding her child for stealing a cookie.

The session Sara and Cathy attended began with Dr. Martin Towner, an educational psychologist from the state of Washington.

"Let me begin by telling you that an expert is someone who lives thirty miles away." He stated.

"This is a little difficult to understand, folks, but stay with me. In the town where you live, there are youth leagues that lease your facilities, right? When you set the rules for them, they wonder what makes you have the credentials to make the rules. To them, you're just another person who lives in their town. They see you at the grocery store or in church. Who are you to tell them what to do? By attending this conference, you have now become someone who lives "thirty miles away." You are not just some local person. You are someone who has credentials."

"Wow, that part about being the expert really rang true with me," Sara said as they walked out of the conference room. "I'll feel so much more confident now when people like Andrea confront me."

"I think I'll check on the other sessions and see what sounds good," Cathy announced.

"I'm meeting you for dinner tonight, so don't plan on any more hanky-panky stuff with your new-found friend," Sara told Cathy as she walked away to another session.

"Works for me," Cathy replied. "I'll meet you at 6 PM in the lounge."

Six o'clock rolled around, and Sara stepped off the elevator onto the main floor and saw Cathy with a good-looking guy by her side.

Cathy beamed, "Oh, hi Sara, meet our new assistant, Eric."

"Our new what?" Sara said, with a look like she swallowed a guppy.

"Oh, I'm just kidding." Cathy cried out. "I was just telling Eric that if he ever got tired of his job in Platsburg, then maybe you would have an opening for him."

"Are we going to dinner?" Sara asked with a bit of anger in her voice.

"Sure. Do you mind if Eric joins us?" Cathy asked, pretending she didn't notice the annoyed look on Sara's face.

"Of course, I don't mind," Sara replied, biting her teeth.

It's a good thing she liked Cathy as much as she did. Cathy was the one person in her life that kept Sara motivated and positive. Her sense of humor and devil-may-care attitude made her the likable person she was. And Sara hoped that this time, maybe, just maybe, her new acquaintance was a better fit than her past few.

*This event happened at a swimming meet in Tampa, Florida, for 12-year-olds.

23

Sara and Cathy arrived back in Torrid Hills full of vim and vigor, ready to take on the challenges of the baseball and soccer seasons. Meanwhile, Arnold continued to work tirelessly with Billy to get him ready for T-ball tryouts. Up every morning before school, Arnold could be heard outside the kitchen window scolding Billy when he dropped the ball. "C'mon Billy!" he would yell, "Damnit, keep your eye on the ball. Now get in the house and get ready for school."

"You're being a little hard on Billy," Sara said as Billy went to his room.

"The only way he's going to make the team is if he doesn't make stupid mistakes," Arnold replied to Sara with a bit of anger.

"Arnold," Sara said in a serious tone. "Billy is five years old. He's going to make mistakes. You'll only make him nervous, and then he may lose confidence. If anyone should understand that, it's you."

Slamming his fist on the table in a fit of anger, Arnold yelled at Sara, "Don't ever criticize me about how I coach Billy. I know what I'm doing!"

Sara sat with her eyes focused on nowhere, wondering if this might be the start of something she dreaded.

Driving to work, Arnold began to think about the blowup he had just had with Sara. Guilt swept over him like a massive tsunami wave approaching the beach.

"This isn't good," he thought to himself. "Sara's right. That's the kind of thing my dad did to me. I've got to watch myself. I refuse to be the "apple" Dr. Monroe warned me about." He spent the day guilt-ridden, trying to get the thought of his outburst at Sara out of his mind.

Arriving home from work, Arnold immediately said to Sara, "I'm sorry for blowing up this morning. You were right. I gotta control myself. I could never forgive myself if I ended up like my father." Sara forgave him right away.

Saturday morning rolled around, and there was a knock on the door.

"Hi, Mr. Jones." came the voice of Billy's friend, Ryan. "Is Billy going to T-Ball today?" Ryan was standing there with his mother, Margaret, who had a pleading look on her face.

"Yes, he is Ryan," Arnold answered. "Are you trying out for T-Ball like Billy?"

"Yep!" Ryan replied. "But my daddy says he's too busy to take me."

"Would he be able to tag along with you two today?" asked Margaret. "I've already filled out the paperwork and signed him up."

"Sure, he can," Arnold replied. "Billy has just finished eating his breakfast, so come on in, Ryan, and we'll be ready to go in a couple of minutes."

"Thanks so much!" Margaret replied as she hugged Ryan. "Have a great time, and I'll see you when you get home." She gave Arnold an appreciative look as she walked out the door.

"Are you excited about playing T-Ball Ryan?" Sara asked.

"Yes!" Ryan said. "But my daddy wants me to play the piano when I get bigger."

"Hi Ryan," Billy said, coming down the stairs dressed for Tee Ball tryouts.

"Are you two ready to go?" Arnold asked with gusto.

The three of them walked to the little league field across the park. Arriving at the field, they caught sight of a sign saying, "Sign-ups"; another said, "Coaches check-in."

"I'm signing up my son, Billy, and his friend Ryan should already be on your list,"

Arnold said to the attendee Melissa Talup.

As he looked toward the "Coaches" sign, there stood his dad, Scotty. As the president of the little league, Scotty was there to witness the tryouts.

"We're going to need coaches, Mr. Jones," Melissa Talup said to Arnold as she put Billy and Ryan's names on the roster of players. "Can we count on you?"

"I haven't coached before. Does it matter?" Arnold said to Melissa.

"Oh, no," Melissa said. "We have a coaches training program, all on video that you can take. And if you pass, you'll be a bonified coach in the program."

"Okay," Arnold replied, feeling he would have no problem becoming "bonified."

The problem might be having to deal with Scotty.

Arnold approached the coach's section after taking Billy and Ryan to the player's section. As he got closer, Scotty yelled over to Billy, "Who's gonna be your coach, Billy? Want me to coach you? Your dad has never played an ounce of baseball worth thinkin' about."

"My dad is gonna sign up to coach, Grandpa," Billy yelled to Scotty, who sat with an ugly grin.

"We'll see, Billy," Scotty said as the players took the field.

Coaches, looking to draft the better players, stood with their clipboards as player after player were asked to show catching and batting skills. Arnold's practice with Billy paid off as he made every catch and hit the ball well off the tee.

Scotty sat there in the stands beaming and announced to anyone who would listen that Billy obviously developed his talent from his grandpa. "Just look at how smooth he is catching the ball." Scotty gleamed. "I swear, he looks just like me out there. He's nothing like his father." he continued, with those around him nodding in agreement like puppets on a string.

An incensed Arnold stood there with a burning desire to break, crush, or destroy Scotty, somehow, someway, someday.

Near the third base, Ryan stood as Rocky Mano threw him the ball over and over. Poor Ryan didn't catch a single one.

"You can have him!" One coach yelled sarcastically.

"He's yours." Answered another coach. *

It was impossible for Ryan not to hear the cruel comments from the insensitive, grown men who would be coaches of the kids who made the team.

He began crying, and with his head hung low and an oversized glove almost touching the ground, he walked over to the bleachers and sat down. "I want to go home," he said when Arnold came to check on him.

As Arnold walked Ryan back home, he couldn't help thinking about the lack of self-worth the little boy was probably feeling and the lost opportunity to have fun and make new friends. All because he couldn't catch a ball.+

"Shame on you guys." Arnold blasted toward the two coaches when he got back. "He's just a little kid who came here only wanting to have fun. I hope you enjoyed what you did to him."

*As heard by a rec professional in Indiana.

24

"Hey Cathy," Sara yelled out across the office. "Did I show you what I'm putting in the brochure to hand out to the coaches and parents at the orientation meeting on Wednesday night?"

"No, what is it?"

"Here, read it and see if you like it."

Cathy took the brochure and read aloud, "At one point during a game, the coach said to one of his players, 'Do you understand what cooperation is? What a team is?' The little boy nodded affirmatively. 'You understand that we play together as a team, Right?' The little boy nodded yes. "So." the coach continued, 'When a strike is called, or you're out at first, you don't argue or curse or attack the umpire. Do you understand that?" Again, the little boy nodded. "Good. Now go over there and explain it to your parents."

"Now that's funny," Cathy said. "And spot on. I can't wait to see the look on parents' faces when they read that Wednesday night."

"I've decided that I'd like you to be the moderator for the soccer league this year," Sara announced to Cathy. "We just need to make sure we don't have any crazies out there."

"Works for me. But I have one request." Cathy responded, looking like a teenager asking her mother to meet her new boyfriend.

"Do you think it would be okay for me to bring Eric every now and then? After all, if anybody gives me a hard time if I threaten them with suspension for bad behavior, Eric could be there to protect me."

"Oh, puleeeez!" Sara answered back dramatically. "I thought that romance was over the first night in Memphis."

"No, it's for real this time. I swear!" Cathy cried out, trying to convince Sara.

"I don't know why I always let you get away with your crazy ideas, but I'll say yes, until the first time I hear a complaint," Sara warned.

"Oh, you're the greatest boss in America," Cathy said, jumping for joy.

"Stop it." Sara rebounded with the look of someone who got swindled by a Mississippi gambler. "Just make sure you are there for the opening game at 9 am Saturday morning."

Cathy and Eric had been seeing each other almost nightly since returning from Memphis. This time it looked like Cathy had finally found, as she put it, The One. Eric was a likable guy. He had starred in basketball at Platburg High School before accepting a scholarship to Boonestown State. After graduating from college, the city of Platsburg, needing a rec department, decided to hire Eric as its director. In two years, he had the city build a complete sports complex with football, soccer, baseball, and softball facilities. He was nominated for Recreation Director of the Year in North Carolina.

Right on schedule, Eric showed up at *Scotty Jones Park* for Saturday's opening soccer match between last year's number one and two teams.

"Hi Eric," Cathy said in a flirty tone.

"Hey there, Ms. Recreation Specialist," Eric said back to her. "So, this is the Scotty Jones Park, huh? Is he here today to watch the opening?"

"No, he's strictly baseball." Cathy shot back.

As the teams lined up to start the game, Cathy took notice of a woman looking extra fidgety on the sidelines. No sooner had the game started than the lady began walking from one end of the sidelines to the other while following her son. All the time screaming and hollering, "Run, Philip, run!" Then as the team got near the goal, she would yell for Philip to kick it in. When she started screaming about the other team's players, calling them weak and dumb, the official took notice. The woman's behavior continued until time out was called by the official in charge of the game. "If you can't control yourself, lady, I'm going to order you off the field." With that, the lady yelled back, "It's my kid out there, and there is no rule that says I can't root him on, so piss off, mister!" She continued to harass the other team's players and yell at Philip to "Slaughter them!". Feeling overly frustrated as the obnoxious behavior continued, the official ran up to her again. "There may not have been a rule before, but I'm creating one now....YOU'RE OUT OF HERE! or the game ends." Full of anger but with no choice, the lady walked out of the park with the crowd booing her.

Soon after, a person on the sidelines approached Cathy, saying, "I know you work for the rec department, so I wanted to know if you saw that man throw his son up against the fence?" *

"Where are they?" Cathy asked with an urgent tone in her voice. The informer pointed out the man, and Cathy hurried toward them with Eric by her side. She approached the man and said, "Is everything okay here, sir?"

"Who the hell are you?" he responded.

"I'm the Assistant Recreation Director. Someone just reported abusive behavior happening over here." Cathy said, feeling her temper rising.

"Mind your own business! You, people, have no jurisdiction over me or anyone else out here, so get off my ass and out of my face." The man yelled at Cathy.

He then grabbed his son by the back of the neck and pushed him hard, saying, "Get your ass to the car!"

Cathy was stunned and said, "Sir, please let's talk about this."

He turned and spat out viciously, "Shut your mouth, bitch!"

Eric could hold back no longer and said, "Don't talk to my girlfriend that way!"

With that, the man took a swing at Eric and missed. Eric grabbed him and threw him to the ground. The police were called, and as they escorted him to the police car, the man turned and said to Cathy, "You just wait until I tell Scotty Jones about this. He'll have your ass out of the rec department in a heartbeat."

Cathy and Eric were both distraught, but they managed to stay calm and help the man's son get his mother on the phone to come pick him up.

On their way back to the rec department office to let Sara know what happened, Cathy suddenly exclaimed, "Wait," and looked over to Eric, "Did I hear you say the word, "girlfriend" back there?"

"I guess it just slipped out," Eric said in a good-natured way as he looked with a blushed face out the window.

"Girlfriend…. I like the sound of that." Cathy said with an oversized grin on her face as they pulled into the rec department parking lot.

The event happened at a soccer field in Greenacres Florida

25

"What in the world have you done now?" Sara said, sounding like a mother dressing down her child for misbehaving in school.

"Did you already hear about it?" Cathy asked, a little surprised.

"The phone's been ringing off the hook with people saying you caused all kinds of ruckus at the game this morning," Sara answered.

"I guess you could call it that. But I'm damn glad I had Eric with me. This jerk threw his son up against the fence because he didn't think he was playing hard enough. I tried talking to him, but he was not about to listen to me. When he pushed his son right in front of us, things kinda escalated. He took a swing at Eric, and Eric had to hold him down until the police showed up. They ended up letting the guy go, though."

"Oh wow," Sara came back. "Is the boy okay?"

"Yeah, his mom came and got him," Cathy answered.

Just then, Sara's cell phone rang. Picking it up to answer, she heard the unmistakable voice of Scotty Jones.

"How can I help you, Scotty?" Sara answered. "No need to start yelling. I know about the disturbance at the soccer field this morning."

"We'll take care of it." Sara continued. "And no, I'm not going to fire my assistant. She was just doing her job.... No. You don't have any power here. When I took this job, I informed Linda Harris, I assume you know Linda, that I would only do so if I had complete charge of all situations...... Well, I suggest that you take your complaint to her. Have a nice day."

Hanging up the phone, Sara began laughing uncontrollably. Struggling to get the words out, she said with a gasping voice, "Oh, how I would love to be a fly on the wall for that conversation!"

After getting control of herself, Sara told Cathy that she better be prepared for a battle at the Wednesday night orientation meeting with the coaches and parents.

"Not to worry," Cathy replied, then turned to head back out. "I just came by to let you know what happened. Eric's waiting in the car. I'll see ya later."

As she got back in her car, Eric said, "Hey, don't forget, my car's back at the field parking lot."

Pulling into the lot, Eric pointed his car out to Cathy. As they got closer, Eric, full of fury, shrieked, "That bastard, he let the air out of my tires!"

Cathy took out her cell phone and took a picture of Eric's flat tires. Across the street, a young kid, looking to be an early teenager, came over and said, "I saw the guy who did that."

"What did he look like?" Eric anxiously asked.

"I'm pretty sure it was Jerry Russo. He had a Blue Devil's shirt on," he told Eric. "He works over at the 7-11 on Lincoln Street."

"Let's go," Eric said to Cathy with a sense of excitement.

"What are you going to do if we find him?" Cathy asked nervously.

"I'm gonna make him fill my tires back up," Eric replied with frustration.

As they reached 7-11, Eric asked Cathy to stay in the car. She decided to pull up her video on her phone in case anything went badly. Eric walked into the store, and no more than ten seconds later, he came running out and hid behind the car. Jerry had a gun and threatened to shoot him.

"Stay down, Cathy!" Eric screamed.

"You keep your ass out of my business, asshole, or the next time this gun goes off," Jerry yelled as customers ran from the store.

Cathy ducked but had captured most of the incident on her phone. Eric climbed into the car, and they sped off to the police department.

"You look like you saw a ghost, Cathy." Officer Mark Summers exclaimed as they walked into the police station.

"Mark, a guy named Jerry Russo, who works at the 7-11 just threatened Eric here with a gun. You need to arrest him." Cathy replied with an urgent tone.

"Do you have any evidence?" Mark asked.

"Right here on video. Look!" Cathy urged Mark.

"No doubt about it." Mark returned, "This is the second time today we've had to deal with him. I'll go down and arrest him myself. I need you two to come along to identify him. This guy has been a problem around here for quite some time. I saw him several times last year when my son, Roger, played. One time he jumped out of the stands, ran out on the field, and punched the umpire after he called his kid out at the plate." *

Eric and Cathy waited outside while Officer Mark dealt with Jerry. When they came out, Jerry was in handcuffs. "Is this the guy?" He asked them as they headed toward the police car.

"It sure is. And ask him if he let the air out of my tires. I'm the one who subdued him at the soccer game this morning." Eric replied angrily.

Jerry wouldn't confess to the tires, but Officer Mark hauled him down to the police station, where he was booked for aggravated assault.

It took most of the afternoon before Eric and Cathy could get Eric's tires back to normal. Needing to head back to Platsburg, Eric said, "Damn, glad we haven't had any of those kinds of nut cases in our programs. You guys need to take a look at what we do to try to keep things under control."

"Now that sounds like an invitation for something to discuss over dinner some night," Cathy said with a pleading sound in her voice.

"How about tonight?" Eric asked.

"Deal!" Cathy responded.

Story told at a youth sports conference in San Antonio, Texas.

26

After the day she just had, Sara decided it might be time to make a visit to her parents for some advice from her mom.

"You look a little weary," Amanda commented when Sara walked in the door. "Is your job keeping you busy?"

"Busy isn't the word, Mom. And these crazy people make the job harder than it should be." She said, feeling tired.

"How so?" Amanda asked.

"Just today, there was a scuffle at the soccer field when a father assaulted his son for not playing up to the father's expectations. With what Arnold went through with his dad, I know how that can affect kids." Sara stated. "What do you tell your client's mom? Do you hear stories of this kind of abuse?"

"Unfortunately, I hear these kinds of stories all the time, Sara." Amanda acknowledged. "But it's not all bad. Just the other day, I was speaking with a client about his son. He started telling me how he had coached a youth football team about 20 years ago. He recently got a call from one of his former players, and the young man asked him to be the best man at his wedding. He said he was dumbfounded and told him that he must have a lot of friends his age to have as his best man; why would he want him? The young man told him that when he was his coach, that it was at a very tough time in his life. His father abused him, and his mother was an alcoholic. He said that as his coach, he was a father figure to him and taught him a lot about the rights and wrongs of getting along in this world. And he had never forgotten." *

"That's very sweet," Sara responded.

"I'm not sure how Arnold is as a coach Sara, but you might want to relate that story to him," Amanda suggested.

Sara stared into space as her mother offered her words of wisdom. She hadn't told her that she worried Arnold might turn out to be like his father. He showed a hint of it earlier before the T-Ball tryouts. What if it gets worse? The thought made chills go up her spine. She had no idea that Arnold himself had been to see Dr. Monroe about the same concerns.

Wanting to change the subject, Sara asked, "How is Dad's practice going?"

"He keeps busy all the time," Amanda replied. "I wish we all could take a vacation sometime. All work and no play…. well, you know the rest."

"Yeah, well, I just thought I'd stop by, Mom," Sara said, walking to the door. "Tell Dad I'm sorry I missed him."

Arriving home, Sara sat in the driveway, watching Arnold and Billy in the backyard. Arnold had placed a "home plate" at the bottom of the elm tree near the back door. He had placed a "first base" about 50 feet away. She sat there for several minutes while Arnold, who sat on an old wooden chair with a stopwatch in hand, was giving instructions to Billy. "Faster this time, Billy," he would yell. Billy panted heavily as the drill went on until he finally begged to stop.

"I'm tired, Dad!" Billy moaned, with Sara watching in disbelief.

"ONE MORE TIME, BILLY. YOU GOT THIS!" Arnold yelled.

Not able to withstand the invective behavior anymore, Sara jumped out of the car and shouted, "Enough, Arnold. Enough!"

With that, Billy ran into the house. Arnold walked hurriedly toward Sara, exclaiming, "What's the matter with you? You just messed up our running practice, damnit!"

"Arnold, Billy is only five years old. You're treating him like he's a fifteen-year-old in high school. You've got to stop trying to make him be something he might not be. You need to let him develop naturally. If you don't, you will push him so hard he could end up hating sports. All because you didn't make his development time a fun experience. So, stop it!"

Arnold wanted to disagree with Sara but knew deep down that she was right. Also, she was the expert in this area and knew what she was talking about.

"I guess you're right," he noted. "I just want to show my dad that Billy is going to be the best player out there on the Tee-Ball field. Maybe that will shut him up."

"And what if he's not Arnold?" Sara feeling like a hissing pot about to boil over. "Will you make fun of him? Will you make him feel worthless? What, Arnold?"

"I don't want to discuss it." Arnold reacted, feeling jilted.

Before dinner that evening, Arnold picked up his cell phone and called Dr. Monroe's office.

"This is Arnold Jones. Is Dr. Monroe available tomorrow?"

Story told by a youth league coach at a coach's clinic in Austin, Texas.

27

Wednesday evening rolled around, and Sara and Cathy were primed and ready to go to the annual orientation meeting for all spring leagues using the *Scotty Jones Park* facilities. Scotty Jones was there, front and center, representing the baseball league. He was extremely annoyed, knowing he would have to listen to Sara announce the rules for the coming season.

Two hundred and thirty-one coaches and parents filled the room. Outside, a few disgruntled parents mulled about while complaining that attendance was mandatory.

"Who the hell does she think she is?'" One woman yelled to anyone who would listen. "We've never had to do this before around here."

"Did you see on that notice they sent? What's with the bit that if we make any kind of protest about an official's call, we have to pay a down payment of one hundred dollars to be heard from the league?" Another person chimed in. "That's bullshit!"

"Yeah, they say you get the hundred dollars back if the league takes your side," A third person added. "but I guarantee it will be rigged, so they can fill their pockets with the money they say we lose."
*

"Last chance for you to come in." Cathy alerted the few remaining outside.

"And what if we don't come in?" Tammy Weston reacted with her face scrunched up.

"Well, that's easy," Cathy replied with a snarky smile on her face. "Your kid won't be on a team this year."

At that, the would-be protesters rushed to get in the door just in time to hear Sara announce that there would be a "no-nonsense policy" this year.

"By that," Sara continued, sounding like a first sergeant at early morning roll call, "I mean we will not put up with any misbehavior like yelling at the game officials or demeaning the coaches. Just look at the 'Behavior Code' brochure Cathy handed out when you came in the door. All the rules are in there."

"Who makes you lord and savior of this league with all these rules?" Scotty blasted out, looking around for support from the crowd.

"I did." Sara countered with a sternness that vibrated through the room with the seriousness of a lion about to pounce on its prey. "And, if anybody doesn't like the rules, then you can ask for your registration fee back and enroll your child in some other activity."

With that, Scotty, snappish as a junk-yard dog, said, "Forget what this woman has to say. I happen to be friends with the Chairman of the Recreation Commission, Linda Harris. We'll get this woman, and her crazy ass rules, out of here in no time."

Sara glanced at Cathy with a wink, then said to Scotty, with a stare that could melt a glacier, "Thank you very much for your comments, Mr. Jones. Please set up a meeting with Mrs. Harris and let me know when I might attend. Until then, folks, you have the rules on the brochure that was handed out. Study the rules well. We aim to have the best youth league program in America here in Torrid Hills."

After some more announcements and more complaints about the changes being made, the meeting ended. The murmur in the room as the attendees filed out the door might have matched the sound of an approaching tornado hovering above Torrid Hills.

While standing next to Cathy, discussing the turmoil Sara had just created, a woman came back in. As she approached Sara, she said, "My name is Melinda Summers. I just want to say that I admire your spunk. No one has ever tried to stand up to all the nonsense we have endured. Coaches have been known to get into physical altercations on the field in front of kids. One parent last year attacked another parent in the parking lot after a game, which sent the woman to the hospital. I couldn't believe what I heard tonight as you stood your ground with Scotty Jones."

"Well, thank you so much," Sara responded, feeling accomplished. "No one likes change, but you could tell from tonight's crowd that changes need to be made."

"Hang in there," Melinda advised Sara as she walked toward the door. "You are not alone in your desire to make the kid's youth league programs one we can all be proud of. And, by the way, if Scotty Jones gives you any problems, don't hesitate to get in touch with me. I can help."

Waiting until Melinda was out the door, Cathy turned to Sara and said with a quizzical look on her face, "What do you suppose she meant by the Scotty Jones remark?"

"I have no idea," Sara answered. "But it's Scotty, so it's probably something bad."

"Well, I have to bolt. I've got a date with Eric." Cathy said to Sara, appearing in a hurry. "I'm meeting him at *Andy's Bar and Grill*. You're welcome to join us if you'd like."

"Thanks, but I think I'll take a rain check." I'm a little worn out after tonight's meeting. I'll see you in the morning."

Cathy arrived at *Andy's* at almost the same time that Eric arrived. "Wow, good timing!" Eric yelled to Cathy as he exited his car. "How was the meeting?"

"I'll tell you about it when we get inside," Cathy replied.

As they entered *Andy's*, they couldn't help seeing Scotty Jones and Jerry Russo sitting in the far corner, looking menacingly at them as they went to the nearest table.

"Should we leave?" Cathy said to Eric.

"Hell no," Eric answered. "They know we're here, and I'll be damned if I want to let them think we are afraid of them."

Not long after Cathy and Eric sat down, Jerry Russo walked over to their table and, looking straight at Eric said, "Don't think I won't get you back for what you did to me, boy."

Eric stood up and replied in a calm but stern manner, "Well, it's good to know you're not only an abusive asshole, you're a racist too."

Cathy grabbed him by his hand and said, "He's not worth it, Eric."

Jerry backed up and turned to walk away, muttering, "Go back to where you belong."

With that, Cathy lunged at Jerry, but Eric grabbed her around the waist to hold her back. He pulled her into their booth, and she landed on his lap. After a minute, she calmed down, looked at Eric's beautiful face, and kissed him.

Eric looked at Cathy with a small smile and said, "I didn't mention it to you before, but when I went to Boonestown, I was the first black person to attend this all-White Baptist College there. I've dealt with bigots like him more times than I can count."

"Well, he and Scotty Jones can go straight to hell, for all I care." Cathy shot back, then kissed Eric again.

This policy is implemented at some rec departments to cut down on frivolous protests of official calls.

28

"Have a seat, Arnold." Dr. Monroe urged as Arnold walked into her office. "I'm a little surprised that you've returned so soon."

After an hour with Dr. Monroe, Arnold had much to think about on his drive home. He had been feeling depressed from the chastisement he had received from Sara. Her telling him that he was showing signs of being abusive to Billy while practicing for the upcoming T-Ball season really hurt.

He thought he was being a good father, urging Billy to build up his speed by making him run over and over. But Sara thought he was obsessed. The worst part is that she said he was acting like his father. 'I'd want to kill myself if that were true.' He thought.

As he pulled out onto the highway, he remembered Sara saying, "When it comes to Billy playing organized sports like T-Ball, there are scoreboards and championships, and we have to be careful not to put undue pressure on him. Sometimes parents can live vicariously through their child. I see it all the time at work. When a kid is called out on a third strike, the parent acts like they are being called out. Or if their kid is not put in the starting lineup, the parent acts like they are humiliated, as if it's a reflection on them."

Arnold stopped at a red light, deep in thought. 'While I understand what she is saying, I can't seem to control my actions.' He said to himself. 'Like continuing to make him run yesterday. Even though I knew I shouldn't do it, I couldn't help myself. My dad has filled me with this uncontrollable pressure to retaliate by making my son better than he was at sports.'

He had discussed a lot of this with Dr. Monroe in their session. But there was no magic pill that she could prescribe. She made Arnold feel like this was going to be a heavy burden he would have to conquer. His father looking over his shoulder and filling him with rage was not going to be healthy. Short of suggesting that he give up coaching T-Ball, which would be a terrible blow, she suggested that he fight hard to avoid the dreaded "apple tree effect ."Arnold knew what she meant.

As he continued toward home, he noticed a large orchard with trees full of blooms. The sign on the road said, *"Welcome to Adam's Apple Orchard."*

29

While running out the door to get to work, Sara caught the eye of her neighbor, Margaret, who was walking her dog.

"Hi Margaret," Sara said with a welcoming voice. "How're things going with Ryan?"

"He decided to take piano lessons and loves it," Margaret responded with relief. "I guess T-ball wasn't his thing. There's going to be a recital on Friday evening. If you guys could make it, I'm sure Ryan would love it, especially if Billy came."

"Well, you can count on us being there," Sara responded with a smile as Margaret continued down the street.

As Sara walked up to the entrance of the rec department, there stood Cathy with her hands on her hips, fidgeting as if she couldn't wait to impart the news she was about to tell.

"Guess who just called the office looking for you?" Cathy said with a smug look on her face.

"Do I want to know?" Sara asked with a bit of apprehension.

"Your best friend, Linda Harris," Cathy replied, knowing Linda was the last person Sara would ever want to hear from.

"What did she want?" Sara responded, sounding like she was looking at bird droppings on her front porch. "Surely she doesn't want to meet with me?"

"Oh, but she does," Cathy answered. "Can I go to the meeting with you?"

"What, and have you get me fired?" Sara jolted back, then smiling, said, "Oh, wait, I forgot, she can't fire me."

"I suggest that you call her and get it over with." Cathy offered.

Pulling out her cell phone as she entered the building, Sara called Linda.

"Hello, this is Sara Jones. Is Linda available? I'm returning her call."

"She'll be right with you." the person on the other end acknowledged.

"This is Linda." She answered. "Can you come to my office Sara? I need to discuss something with you that can't be done over the phone."

"Well, okay," Sara replied, anticipating and wondering what Linda wanted to discuss that couldn't be done over the phone. "I'll be right over."

"Can I go? Can I go?" Cathy badgered Sara, half sounding as if she were a child wanting to go to a theme park, the other half as if she were serious.

"No, you can't." Sara retorted, her face cringing up. "This could be something serious."

Sara brushed her hair back as she looked in her car mirror, wanting to appear her best in front of Linda.

Linda had been working at the Torrid Hills Country Club when she first met her husband, Bernard Harris. He was the mayor of Torrid Hills, but he was also an avid golfer. He would often stay after his round and sit at the bar just to get a chance to talk to Linda. It didn't take long before the two started dating, and soon they eloped. They had two children, who were now nine and thirteen.

"Good afternoon." The lady at the desk announced as Sara walked into Linda's office. "Linda is waiting to see you in her office."

"Hello, Sara," Linda said with a darting gaze, not wanting to look Sara in the eye. "Please close the door and have a seat."

"Let me get straight to the point." Linda declared. "I'm quite aware that you have kept the dalliance between Scotty and me to yourself, and I appreciate that. But recently, things have become more serious. My husband is threatening a divorce. We have been fighting for the past few years, and he "wants out," as he put it. If he were to have any knowledge of the relationship between Scotty and me, I'm sure the divorce could never be contested. He might get the kids, and I would be out on my own."

"And you are telling me this because?" Sara questioned Linda, thinking that Linda might either be threatening her or offering her money for the video. Her guess was verified as Linda replied, "I was thinking of offering you some money if you would delete the video."

"Not a chance," Sara answered so sternly that she feared her voice might have been heard through the walls.

"Perhaps if it were just you, I might take you up on your offer. But, with the other person being Scotty Jones, I wouldn't begin to consider it."

"I'm sorry you feel that way about Scotty, Sara," Linda said, glaring at her. "You do know that Scotty has friends? I assume you heard how one of those friends made your husband forget he even saw Scotty and me at the hotel in Greensboro? I certainly hope that one of Scotty's friends doesn't pay you a visit too. I'm just saying."

"Your threat, if that's what it is, doesn't bother me, Linda," Sara said, grinding her teeth as her face reddened. "Keep in mind that the video is in a safe place where only one other person knows its whereabouts. I'm sure, under your new circumstances, that you would not want the video to become available to not only your husband but to all of Torrid Hills." Sara blasted as she stood up and walked to the door. Turning toward Linda, she continued, "Never threaten me again. I could slice you down like a cold piece of meat before you could whisper *mercy.*"

Linda sat stunned at Sara's countering threat. As Sara stormed out the door, Linda picked up her phone and called Scotty.

30

"I guess things are going okay over there at the rec department," Emma asked over the phone to Sara. "Hell, I haven't heard from you for what seems forever."

"Well, if anyone knows the struggles I have to contend with around these crazies at the ballpark, it's you, Emma," Sara responded. "The season starts next week for baseball and soccer. We have a record number of entries in both programs. But I'm glad you called. I meant to call you about an issue I had the other night after a contentious orientation meeting with the parents. First, Scotty Jones is going to be a pain in the butt. Arnold is going to be coaching our son, Billy, and already it's become a problem."

"Oh, no, poor Arnold," Emma exclaimed. "With Scotty having the field named after him, it gives him this superior attitude. He's like the fox guarding the chicken house. And with Arnold being one of the chickens, nothing good is going to come from it."

"You've got that right," Sara said with exasperation. "I did have something else I wanted to ask you about. Have you ever heard the name Melinda Summers?"

"Oh, sure," Emma replied. "She's a friend of mine. I guess you don't keep up with the local politics around Torrid Hills. She's actually one of the city council members who was strongly against naming the park after Scotty, partly due to his deplorable behavior at ball games."

"Well, I guess that's why she came up to me after the meeting to congratulate me for standing up to Scotty and said not to worry about him. That people like him don't get away with their awful behavior forever. Then she said, 'You'll see.' I was wondering what she meant by that."

"Interesting," Emma said as she looked toward the ceiling in her office. "When I first moved here, it was well known that Scotty was a womanizer. I don't think he would have married her if Martha hadn't gotten pregnant with Arnold. Some say that the reason Scotty is so mean to Arnold is because he never wanted a child in the first place. Apparently, he and Martha fight all the time. I'm sure you've witnessed it. The rumor is Scotty doesn't want to ruin his reputation as a 'good family man,' so he and Martha remain married."

"So, how does Melinda enter the picture?" Sara asked, trying to figure out what Emma would tell her.

"That's the really crazy part." Emma continued. "When Melinda first came to town, we became friends. One night we were out at *Andy's,* and she told me about this guy that was giving her the creeps. Guess who that was? Apparently, Scotty had spotted her at the local convenience store and began a conversation. Knowing she was single was all he needed. He got her number somehow, and night after night, he would call, asking her to meet him at some secluded spot. She refused, but Scotty wouldn't give up. One night, as she left work, he followed her in his car. When she first spotted him in her rearview mirror, she thought it was a coincidence. But she realized he was following her every move, so she began to speed up. He sped up, too, chasing her as she tried to make it home. When she saw the traffic light ahead turn red, she put on her brake. But Scotty didn't see her slow down and plowed into the back of her car, causing it to lunge forward and run headfirst into a tree. Melinda was knocked unconscious. When she came to, she lay bleeding with her head over the steering wheel. The police were there, and when they questioned Melinda as to what had happened, she explained that someone was stalking her, and she had tried to get away. She didn't remember how she had hit the tree at the time. It was all a blur. When asked to identify her stalker, she said, 'Scotty Jones.' And here's where the story gets more interesting." Emma went on with some suspense in her voice. "When Melinda stated that it was Scotty, the police officer said, 'Oh, that couldn't be. Scotty is one of our upstanding citizens. He would never stoop to stalking someone.' Melinda was torn apart with seemingly no recourse. She said after a couple of days, she remembered him plowing into the back of her car and hitting the tree, but with the way this town is and all of Scotty's cronies on his side, she didn't think she had any case against him. It was her word against his."

"Wow. That's some story," Sara mused.

"So now you have an ally." Emma acknowledged. "Trust me, she's looking for any excuse to take him down."

"Thanks for sharing that, Emma," Sara remarked. "I have a lot to think about. And I have a lot to do! I better go."

"Let's try to keep more in touch," Emma replied before they hung up.

For the remainder of the day, Sara, most of the rec staff, and the maintenance crew worked on the preparations needed for the opening ceremony for spring sports in Torrid Hills.

31

Over at Scotty Jones Park, Cathy scurried around like a loose hungry chicken looking for kernels of corn. She was hell-bent on making sure everything was in place for the opening ceremonies of the Torrid Hills Baseball League. As the stands began to fill, situated on the well-groomed infield stood the Torrid Hills High School band. You'd have thought they were headliners for this year's Macy's Day Parade as the brass section stood nervously, fidgeting with their newly polished instruments. A few restless band members practiced blowing offkey notes just to make sure their instruments worked. Rufus Jameson's son Ringo brought the crowd to a roar of laughter with his tuba as it made the sound of a humongous fart. Waiting for a signal from Cathy, the high schoolers stood ready to play the national anthem as the last of the town locals found their seats. An event like this was a big deal in Torrid Hills. Homemade banners, flying around like they were caught in a windstorm, flew all over the place promoting each team. Squirming players stood nervously, crossing and uncrossing their arms, shouting in high-pitched voices at one another, impatient for the event to get underway. Arnold sat in the front row feeling as if someone had taken a vegetable peeler to his nerves. This T-Ball season would be his chance to show his father that he had done an excellent job getting Billy ready. He couldn't fail.

The band hit the first note of the Star-Spangled Banner. Surprisingly, only a little bit offkey. The crowd jumped to its feet in stark unison, as if someone had announced the President of the United States had suddenly arrived. Parents and well-wishers standing tall placed their hands over their hearts showing devout patriotism as only in middle America.

Sara beamed as if she were ready to conquer the world. Over the screeching sound of the speaker system, Sara yelled, "WELCOME TO TORRID HILLS LITTLE LEAGUE SEASON," causing Eric, who was sitting in the stands with Cathy, to say jokingly, "People in my town of Platsburg might have heard that!"

With the announcing of the beginning of baseball season in Torrid Hills, Sara had no choice but to invite her father-in-law and park namesake Scotty Jones to come up to the pitcher's mound to throw the "official first pitch" to Mayor Bernard Harris. Watching them, Sara thought, 'If the poor mayor knew what I know, he wouldn't have that big smile on his face right now.'

Tradition called for the baseball league to have the President offer a few words of wisdom to the audience, so Sara begrudgingly invited Scotty to the microphone.

"It is my pleasure to be your president for this coming year," Scotty proclaimed, sounding like Patrick Henry himself, giving his 'Give me liberty or give me death' speech. "I don't think anyone with such a distinguished record as mine has been in this position before. May the good Lord lead me as I offer my helpful insights to make this year's program a success….."

As the audience began squirming after several minutes of Scotty's meandering about his accomplishments, Sara found the perfect time to jump in. Once Scotty had resorted to taking a breath, Sara leaned toward the mic and said, "Thank you very much, Scotty," and then turned to the band for their final number. Looking like he had been handed a hot iron from an ironing board, Scotty turned with a scornful face toward Sara and said resentfully, "Nice move."

As the band blared out its version of the Hallelujah Chorus loud enough for the Lord in Heaven to hear, the crowd drifted from the field, mumbling how their team would crush the others this season. Cathy and Eric came up to the stage to congratulate Sara on a job well done, leaving Cathy to add, "I think you might have pissed Scotty off a bit."

"You think so?" Sara replied, looking half pissed off herself. "He is so egotistical that if I didn't cut him off, he would still be out there rambling on."

Just then, Arnold and Billy walked up to them. "How about we all go for pizza?" Arnold suggested. "You and Eric are welcome to join us, Cathy."

"That sounds like a great idea!" Cathy replied, looking at Eric, who nodded enthusiastically.

The five of them laughing and enjoying pizza were just what Sara and Arnold needed to get Scotty out of their heads.

32

"The event today reminded me that your department was named the best recreation program in America." Cathy said to Eric as they sat down in a booth at *Andy's* after pizza night with the Jones'. "Are there any specific things you guys did that earned you that honor?"

"Yep, we decided that after all the problems we were having with coaches, we would create a mandatory training program. It seemed crazy that teachers have to go through four years of college to qualify to teach kids in the classroom, but the same kids can have somebody with no training out on the field or court with them. Sports seasons last an average of 8 weeks, and these kids are learning a lot about life. I feel that the sports fields are the outdoor classroom."

"I bet making it a requirement went over like a led balloon," Cathy said, laughing.

"You're right," Eric responded. "They threatened to get me canned. The mayor was one of the football program coaches and came to my house to tell me if I made the program mandatory, I would be fired."

Looking directly into Eric's eyes, Cathy leaned forward and said, "So what did you do?"

"I said to the mayor, 'Oh, don't worry. You don't have to go to the training program. It's just that whoever doesn't go forfeits their chance to qualify for the championship.' He looked at me as if he wanted to hit me over the head with the closest board he could find."

"Man, that was a great idea. Did they all show up for the program?" Cathy replied.

"Yep. And not only that, one guy stood up at the end and said, 'Why haven't we done this before?'" Eric said proudly.

"What was the training program all about?" Cathy asked.

"We kept it simple. We had an EMT talk about what to do if someone gets injured, and then a local child psychologist talked about the role of winning in kids' sports. You wouldn't believe how they got into it when she asked them to discuss what they thought about 'winning at all costs.' After the program was over, a guy came walking up to me with this scowl on his face. I thought he was going to chew me out for making him come to the program. But I was shocked when he blurted out, 'Do you think I should be a coach?' He had the strangest look on his face. I asked him, 'Why do you ask me that?' He then floored me with his next statement. He said, 'When I heard the lady talking about all the things that happen to kids when you preach win at all cost, I thought of all the things I have done in the past. That's why I don't know if I should still be a coach.' I said to him, 'With that statement, you're showing me that this program has done what it's supposed to do. You should still coach. You now know what it's all about.' I thought that was the end of it until after he took a few steps away, he turned to me and said, 'I've damaged a lot of kids.' I stood there stunned." *

Cathy sat staring at Eric admiringly and said, "Now that's impressive. No wonder you got the award you received. I can't wait to tell Sara about what you did. I guarantee you, she will want to do a similar program."

"Hey, not to change the subject, but Scotty Jones is staring at us right now," Cathy said, looking annoyed. "Sara told me she thinks Scotty is a racist and doesn't like the idea of you and me being together."

"Well, that's his damn problem. If he doesn't like it, let him come tell me himself."

"Yeah, he is a total jerk. I feel bad for Sara," Cathy said. "And especially Arnold. He is so obsessed with Arnold. You just watch. There's going to be a blow-up between the two before the season is over. You can only boil the water for so long before it boils over."

Changing the subject again, Cathy said, "So, I was thinking since you may not want to head back to Platsburg now, we could ride up to Bold Alley Ridge and watch the sunset."

"Are you suggesting that you and I go up and just sit there, or do you have something else in mind?"

"Now, Eric, why would you ever think I would have something else in mind?" Cathy teased as a look of intense amorousness spread over her face like water released suddenly from a broken dam.

*This story was told to the author at a coach's clinic.

33

In Torrid Hills, no matter what the weather, warm, cold, rain or shine, the first Saturday of spring is also unofficially the first day of "little league baseball." Many kids have waited impatiently for the day when they can wear their shoes, uniform, and newly worked in baseball gloves and head to their first game at the local park. For Billy Jones, it would be his first go-around of what was to be an adventure he didn't expect.

"Time to get up, Billy. It's the big day we've been waiting for!" Arnold cried out. Sara looked out the kitchen window. Daffodils and pansies were about to burst out of their buds. Billy loved the pansies the best. When he was three years old, he and Sara would walk around the yard and pick the petals from the flowers and say, "She loves me, she loves me not." The idea of picking daises and the "she loves me" ditty Sara had learned from her mother, who learned it from her mother, had her feeling nostalgic. So now Billy would have the time-worn tradition to pass along. Sara was careful to always have the last petal say, "She loves me." Billy never caught on, but he loved knowing his mother "loved him."

"Gotta have a big breakfast this morning," Arnold demanded of Billy. Sounding like the professional coach he recently saw on TV, he continued, "Being a top-notch athlete means that you take good care of your body. And starting the day off right means eating a healthy breakfast."

"What's a top-notch athlete, Dad?" Billy asked with his face scrunching up.

Arnold looked at Sara, hoping she could help explain.

153

"It means you are a good athlete, Billy," Sara said. "You know how you and your dad have been practicing throwing and catching and running in the backyard? Well, that's because he wants you to be a top-notch baseball player."

"What if I'm not?" Billy responded.

Before Sara could say a word, Arnold jumped in and said, "Don't say that, Billy. You are a good baseball player, and we're going to show everybody that you're the best. Okay?"

"I guess so," Billy answered with a quizzical look on his face. "I just hope it's fun."

"Hurry up and finish your breakfast. We want to make sure we're the first to get to the field." Arnold said.

If there was pressure on Billy to attend his first T-Ball game, it didn't show as he played with his toy dinosaurs, lining them up one by one. As for Arnold, that was a different story. The thought of Billy not meeting Arnold's expectations left a pit in his stomach. Imagining his father sitting in the stands, with his eyes burning a hole in him, made Arnold feel as if he were standing on a frozen pond, forced to go forward, not knowing how thick the ice was.

Since the T-Ball field was within walking distance, Arnold told Sara that he and Billy would walk and talk strategy. Sara cringed when she heard Arnold say the word "strategy."

"Arnold," she reacted, "just remember, Billy will be just six years old in a few days. You might as well be talking to him in Greek when you used the word strategy."

"I know what I'm doing." Arnold snapped, insulted at the thought that he didn't know how to be Billy's coach.

Sara bristled when hearing Arnold's tone. "I hope so. This is about Billy having fun. Don't forget that." She snapped back at him.

Seeing Arnold and Billy walking down the road to the field, Sara felt a sense of guilt at the way she had just handled that with Arnold. At the end of the day, it was Arnold who was under immense pressure to overcome his childhood suffering at the hands of Scotty. He would have to overcome those torments, and maybe coaching would provide the "medicine" to do so.

As Arnold and Billy walked the brick-lined path to the field, Arnold began with the "strategy."

"So, here's the thing, Billy," Arnold said urgently. "When you get up to bat, remember to keep your eyes on the ball when you swing the bat. When you're in the infield, make sure you always keep your eyes on the ball when the hitter hits it. And, most important, If the ball comes to you, look around to see if anyone else is on base. If so, make sure you throw it to the person where there is no one from the other team on base. You got it?"

"Do those pansies over there grow all year round, Dad? I like it when mom and I play, 'she loves me, she loves me not.'" Billy asked, happily enjoying the walk.

"Did you not hear a word I was telling you?" Arnold asked impatiently.

"Huh?" Billy answered as he gazed up to the sky to look at the plane roaring overhead like it did at the same time every day.

A knot tightened in Arnold's stomach as he and Billy neared the field. Sitting alone in the bleachers was the one person he feared would ruin the day for him and Billy.

34

"Hi, Mom," Sara said. "Fancy seeing you in my office first thing in the morning. What gives?"

"Since Billy's first T-Ball game is today, I thought I'd stop by to see if you would be going," Amanda said to Sara. "I remember the first time you played soccer. I loved seeing you out there enjoying yourself."

"I can't go, I have to work, but Cathy will be there," Sara replied. "It's her job to go to games and watch the behavior of the parents and coaches."

"Has Arnold been pushing Billy hard to get ready for this game?" Amanda asked with concern.

"No, no," Sara replied, wanting to change the subject.

"Hey, Cathy," Sara yelled to Cathy, sitting down the hall in her office. "Do you mind if my mom goes to the game with you this morning?"

"She's such a pain to be around. I'd rather go by myself." Cathy responded, trying to start the day off with her wry sense of humor.

"She says she feels the same way about you," Sara said, trying to match Cathy's wit.

"Oh, hi Amanda." Cathy quipped as she rounded the corner to see Amanda sitting in Sara's office. "Gee, I didn't know you were here."

"Okay, enough with the joking around," Sara said. "I think it's great that you two can go together to the game. That way, we'll get a double opinion as to how things go."

157

Walking out the door, Cathy turned to Sara and said, "You never told me being a babysitter to your mom was part of the job."

Cathy and Amanda hit it off from the first time they met at the *Bowlerama* when Cathy was put on the Tobin's team. Unfortunately, Cathy Ellerson was no gift to the bowling world. In the first game, she bowled; her score was a whopping twenty-seven. The word around the other teams that night was that her score might just well have been the lowest in Torrid Hills bowling history. All eyes were on her lane throughout the first night as she struggled to get the bowling ball out of her hands. She gripped the ball as if it were filled with dynamite and threw it down the lane like she couldn't wait to get rid of it. You'd have thought she was having the worst time of her life; that is until she broke out in her own distinct roaring laughter that some said sounded like a hyena. Others thought it had the sound of someone screaming in agony. At any rate, she was the source of entertainment on the opening night. As the season went on, the Whacos team ended in last place, but the crowd's willingness to laugh along with Cathy made it fun for all. In her final announcement to the other league members, Amanda suggested Cathy try the Torrid Hills Sewing Society the following year, thus ending the night with a roar of laughter.

"I'm so glad you're going to the game with me, "Cathy said to Amanda as they walked down the tree-lined path adjacent to Manford Street. "I'd like to hear your thoughts after you see how excited parents can get watching their child play organized sports for the first time. It just seems like something surreal, how protective some of them can be."

"When kids play sports," Amanda replied. "Most parents want everything to go right for them. Some parents can control their emotions, but others have a harder time."

"Yeah," Cathy responded, "In this country, we glorify sports. It's all over TV with all-star games, super bowls, you name it. Some parents will stop at nothing to see their son or daughter make it to the highest level in sports. They will send them to sports camps and even pay thousands of dollars for them to play in tournaments."

"Yes," Amanda agreed, "and anything that stands in the way of that can cause their emotions to rise. I remember hearing Arthur Ashe, the famous tennis player, talking about one of his teammates in college. He said this one teammate's parents made him get up early every morning before school and practice tennis for two hours. Arthur said that when the team played its last tennis match, that kid put his racquet down and never played again."

"I could see that happening with some of the kids that are in our programs," Cathy said with a disappointed tone.

"It's all about trying to keep things in perspective," Amanda replied.

As they reached the ballfield, parents were filling the stands skittishly, mumbling among themselves in anticipation of the game starting. Kids were dressed in uniforms, with one team's shirts adorned with the 'Bluebirds' and the other team, the 'Rockets.' Arnold Jones paced nervously in the dugout on the third base side. Billy followed him up and down the dugout as if he feared that Arnold would desert him.

As they took their seats, Amanda looked over to where Billy stood, fidgeting with his ballcap. Billy caught sight of her and Cathy, and looking like a child stranded on an island, he waved beggingly, hoping the two would come to rescue him.

In the bleachers' back row was Scotty Jones peering down on the ballfield like an eagle about to pounce on its prey. The prey, of course, was Arnold. The wrath of Scotty was sure to fall on Arnold should Billy fail to live up to Scotty's expectations.

Amanda turned and nodded disinterestedly but politely toward Scotty. She was well aware of Scotty's belittlement of Arnold over the years. Billy, being her grandson, gave her cause for concern.

"It is silly to think that these kids out there are playing real baseball," Amanda said to Cathy. "Heck, most just learned how to tie their shoes."

As the Rockets began to take the field, half the kids had no idea where to go and what to do when they got there. Fathers grabbed their kids by the arm and led them to their assigned positions. They remained frozen in their infield spaces, hesitant to take even the tiniest step. One of the three kids designated to the outfield stood tilting back and forth like a human pendulum, another leaned over and scraped his hand around an ant pile, while the third, whose ball cap was two sizes too big, covered his eyes from the blinding sun's rays.

Walter Chambly had agreed to be the umpire for today's game. The rec department had recruited any adults they could find to act as volunteer umpires. It was a fun job unless, of course, there was any reason to disagree with the umpires' decisions. And that would be most likely to happen. You just didn't know when.

Ralphie McConnell was the first to bat. The head coach of the other team, Mac Noddjewl, thought Ralphie might be a good hitter and selected him to be the first up at the tee. Sure enough, Ralphie hit a screamer off the tee and into the outfield in Billy's direction. Ralphie, running as fast as he could, rounded first base and then second. All the while, Billy stood holding the ball as if it were a foreign object. "Throw it, BILLY!" Arnold and everyone in the stands yelled in a pitched voice, "THROW IT, THROW IT!" When Ralphie approached third base, his father came running out to the field to guide Ralphie toward home plate. The crowd from the other team and Ralphie's dad began screaming, "Ralphie, go home, go home!" At that, with Billy still holding the ball, looking like a scared rabbit, Ralphie, equally confused by the crowd's chant to go home, began running out of the field and down the street toward his house.

Thus began Billy's first introduction to the world of "little league" baseball. As Amanda had described to Cathy, "This isn't baseball. It is more like a three-ring circus!"

Even Scotty Jones couldn't get angry.

35

Arnold and Billy thankfully made it through the T-Ball season with little interference from Scotty. Trying to figure out how to criticize Arnold and his coaching of Billy didn't seem to interest Scotty much anymore. In the end, T-Ball wasn't really baseball. It was more like uncontrolled bedlam. Billy's baseball skills seemed to improve throughout the season, much to the surprise and delight of Arnold. Next year, however, Billy would be playing in the 6–8-year-old "little league" division where in Torrid Hills, kids played in the *Coach Pitch* program. Arnold faced the problem of having to throw the ball over the home plate to the batters.

Football and soccer seasons began in the fall. The crazy season, Sara would call it. While soccer had its characters, somehow the sport of football brought out the "machos," Sara reminded Cathy as they sat in their favorite corner at *Andy's* for their after-work beer.

Standing at the bar were a group of Torrid Hills's old-time footballers focused on everyone's favorite college and professional football teams. Almost nightly, to their wives chagrin, they stopped at *Andy's* before going home. After a couple of cold ones, their voices went up a few decibels as bragging rights began around the Torrid Hill Youth Football League. In the group were an inordinate number of *Torrid Hill High* former players who prided themselves as coaches. You'd have thought some of them were head coaches at number-one colleges or even the pros from how they talked strategy. Anthony Delicato was one of them. He acted like his team won the Super Bowl the previous season as he stood, boasting about their success. With the bravado of a five-star general, he proclaimed, "I guarantee we will repeat it this year because I've got Charlie Dobrinski back again. He won't turn 12 until after the season is over."

"Yeah? Well, I saw him the other day, and he looked like he put on about thirty pounds over the summer." Ronaldo Tanton bristled in return.

"Not to worry," Anthony replied. "We'll get him down to weight come weigh-in time."

Sara and Cathy could hardly contain themselves as they painfully endured the boastful trash talk among the group.

Before long, Cathy suggested that they might be pressing their luck by staying. The subject of the coaches training program might come up, and they would surely be confronted by the group. Soon after learning about Eric's rec department implementing a training program for coaches in Platsburg, Sara was convinced that her department should do the same. The coaches in Torrid Hills weren't happy. And they stood only a few feet away.

"Thank heavens Scotty Jones isn't among them." Cathy blurted out as she and Sara stood to leave.

"Well, if he were, I'd have been out of here in a flash," Sara responded.

As serendipity would present itself, the man himself walked in the door.

"Hello, Scotty." Sara and Cathy both said in unison as they passed him.

"I'll be bringing up your coaches' training program tomorrow night at the coaches' meeting," Scotty said, never taking the time to recognize the two.

"Sounds good," Sara said. Only a fool would not capture the sarcasm in her voice.

Seated at the front table for the coaches' meeting and reading from the new brochure Sara had created for the upcoming season, Scotty Jones spoke out, saying, "I think it is bullshit that we have to go to this coach's certification program. Hell, I'm a volunteer. Why should I have to go? I think if you played football at Torrid Hill's High, and starred like me, then you wouldn't have to go. What the hell can they teach me, anyway? And while I'm at it, I happened to have been honored with this park being named after me. It's an insult to one of Torrid Hills' famous citizens. Don't you agree?"

To Scotty's dismay, eighty-seven coaches signed up for the training program since Sara made the program mandatory. Like Eric's program, she also stipulated that if your team did not have all its coaches certified, they would not be eligible for the championship. It pissed off all the coaches, but they all planned to attend.

"Better hurry up," Sara yelled to Arnold, who scurried around to find a notepad for the coach's certification program.

"Maybe I should take a baseball bat with me to defend you against the rowdy crowd tonight. There's been a lot of angry talk out there, stirred up mainly by my father. I'm anxious to see what kind of shit he creates."

"Not to worry. He knows better than to raise a ruckus. I'll report him to the head of the rec commission. You know who that is, right?" Sara winked as her eyebrows rose, and a smile that looked like she was posing for a family photo filled her face.

"Yeah, but I think she cares about all of that more than he does. He'll send a goon if he feels threatened. My father is pretty much uncontrollable and untouchable. I don't think anything could bring him down." Arnold said with some despair. "But let's forget about him. I'm excited to learn about how to be a better coach. Let's go!"

The coach's certification program was a great success. Not one coach in Torrid Hills opted to stay away. At the urging of Cathy, Eric agreed to be the moderator for the program. He started with a video showing excerpts of how the coaches in Platsburg reacted to the program. Most said it made them appreciate their role in helping kids have fun first. Dr. Tobin, Sara's dad, was there to review first aid's importance. Wally Turner, who owned the only McDonalds in town, told David Riggers, "I'm damn glad Doc Tobin was there to talk about dealing with injuries. I never thought how important it was to have a first aid kit. I'll tell you one thing. I had a lot of kids get banged up during practice, like skinned knees and elbows. I just shrugged it off and told them to toughen up."

A week later, it was time for the football orientation meeting at the Torrid Hills High School gym. All football coaches had to attend. It was a time when they would hand out the game schedules and review any new rules the league had agreed to implement. Ellie Robins, the league secretary, handed out the *Torrid Hills Football League Guidelines* to all the coaches as they entered the building. The *Guidelines* spelled out the rules for the league. One that was very clear was the weight limits. Players running the ball had to be under a certain weight, depending on their age division. The *Guidelines* stated there would be a weigh-in on the Friday before the season began.

One hundred and seventy kids signed up for football on August 20th, the first day for signups. Sara and Cathy sat at the sign-in tables and collected registration fees along with the doctor's certificates stating players were fit to play. When Anthony Delicato sighted Charlie Dobrinski at the signups, he gulped. Ronaldo Tanton was right. Charlie had put on considerable weight over the summer.

"Get your butt to practice the first thing next week, Charlie." Anthony demanded. "I need to see how much you weigh."

When Charlie arrived for practice the following Monday, Anthony stood with a bathroom scale ready to weigh him in.

"Damn, Charlie," Anthony cried out as if he'd seen an oversized monster. "You shot up to one hundred and forty pounds. The max weight for the 9- to 11-year-old division is one hundred and twenty pounds! How are we going to ever get you at quarterback this season?"

Looking like he swallowed a canary, Charlie replied, "I can get down to one-twenty coach. Once practice starts, it will come off."

"We can't afford to lose you at quarterback, Charlie, so let's get at it, starting today."

The season would begin a week from Saturday, and weigh-ins would be held the day before. Each day at practice, Anthony had the scales out to weigh Charlie. The bad news was that he was still ten pounds overweight with one week to go. So, Anthony had a plan. He knew most of the weight was from the water in the body. On Friday before practice, he began his plan. It was a hot North Carolina day, with temperatures hovering around ninety degrees. Little did Anthony know that Charlie's mother, Abigail, had scheduled a dentist's appointment for him after practice. She arrived early to watch Charlie. Looking throughout the field of players, she didn't spot him. Starting to worry, she eyed Coach Anthony and, with a concerned look, said, "I don't see Charlie, coach. Did he skip practice?"

"Oh, no Mrs. Dobrinski. He's in the car over there getting down to weight before tomorrow's weigh-in. You know how bad we need him this season."

As Abagail walked to the car, she could hear the engine running. Wide-eyed, she opened the door. There sat Charlie, wrapped from head to toe in plastic wrap. The heat was running full blast, while Charlie sat with salted sweat pouring down his face as red as a beat.

"OH, MY LORD," Abagail screamed in horror. "Get out of the car Charlie, NOW!... Before you pass out."

Coach Anthony ran over to the car, crying, "WHAT HAPPENED?"

"What happened? What happened!?" Abigail hollered at the coach. "You could have killed my son. That's what happened! He could have died from heat stroke if I hadn't been here. Are you an idiot? Get in the car, Charlie. You'll never play football with this ridiculous idiot again."

As Charlie stepped to get into the car, he fell to the ground, and panic set in, "Call an ambulance!" one of the coaches yelled.

"What do we do?" Anthony shrieked.

"Grab the ice out of the cooler." Another coach suggested. "Throw some cold towels on him."

The sirens from the ambulance got closer as everyone ran around in a panic wondering if Charlie would make it. Abagail stood helplessly in shock.

The paramedics jumped out of the ambulance and began their procedure for bringing Charlie back to consciousness. Their experience worked, and soon he was awake with cold compresses covering his body. While the paramedics loaded Charlie in the ambulance, Abagail stared at Anthony with eyes so menacing it would scare a lion.

"You'll be hearing from my lawyer," she warned as she hurried to her car to follow the ambulance.

36

Western Carolina has its share of joyless cold and snowy winters. Joyless for adults, that is, who are forced to plow their way out of driveways while struggling to get to work. All the while, kids, seeing the first snowflake of the year, would scream, "IT'S SNOWING!" .... It was time for Brandywine Hill.

On February 15th, a bumper winter storm swept its way up the east coast like a ferocious snowy tsunami. Snow piled up so deep that cars, looking like abandoned caskets, sat motionless in driveways throughout Torrid Hills. Sara's dad, Dr. Tobin, had his share of heart attack patients who had succumbed to the arduous task of hopelessly shoveling snow out of their driveways.

Billy could hardly contain himself. "Dad," he cried out, fearing the worst from his father Arnold's response, "Can I go sled riding, PLEASE? All my friends from school will be over at Brandywine Hill today."

"We talked about this before, Billy," Arnold responded as Billy sat on his bedside, unable to hold the tears. "There will be hundreds of kids up there on the mountain. All it will take is one kid to plow into you, and your baseball season will be over. We can't risk it."

Washing dishes in the other room, Sara overheard the conversation and quietly said, "Arnold, can you come into the kitchen for a minute? I need your help with something."

With a look on her face that mirrored a clenched fist, Sara said to Arnold, "Please close the door."

"Why would you ever deny Billy the chance to do something that he can only do a few times in his childhood?" Sara began angrily. "It's cruel. It sounds like something your father would have done to you. And to use the excuse that he might get injured. That's ridiculous. Kids are kids. They always risk injury. You go in there and tell Billy it's okay to go to Brandywine Hill with the other kids. And if you can't take him, I will."

Arnold stood looking at Sara, like a puppy scolded for peeing on the floor for the first time. Sara's words went through him like a matador's final sword thrust.

"You take him," Arnold demanded as the vision of apples falling from a tree consumed him. "I'm going to go lay down."

"Your dad doesn't feel well, Billy, so I'll take you to Brandywine," Sara said as she entered his room where Billy stood, with his tearful eyes turning to eyes as big as joyful saucers.

"Thank you, Mom!" Billy said with excitement, "But wait, I don't have a sled. What am I gonna do?"

"That's okay, Billy," Sara said reassuringly, "We'll stop by the store on the way and pick one up for you."

Coming out of the store, Sara thought to give Cathy a call. "Hey, Cathy. Since there's not much we can do at the office, how'd you like to play in the snow today?"

"Well, that sounds like an order I can't refuse?" Cathy replied as she fumbled with the cell phone in her hand. "I was just going to call Eric to see if he can get out of the snow in Platburg and come over since their office is closed today."

"Billy's dying to go sledding, and Arnold's not feeling well, so I was hoping you two might join us," Sara responded. "I'm sure I'll need a break going up and down the hill."

"Oh, we can do that," Cathy reacted. "I'm sure Eric would love sledding with Billy. Too bad Arnold can't be there. That's a dad thing that only comes a few times in a lifetime."

"Yeah, hopefully, we'll get another snow day this winter." Sara continued, "Okay, I'll meet you at the hill in about ten minutes.

"Works for me!" Cathy said.

When Sara and Billy arrived at the park, it didn't surprise Sara to see hundreds of people coming up and down the hill in all kinds of contraptions. People of all ages were there with their sleds, saucers, blown-up inner tubes, or any device they could assemble. Billy's friend, Jackie Longo, took the cardboard box his mother's refrigerator came in and shaped it like a navy destroyer. From a drone's view, Brandywine Hill looked like a colony of penguins enjoying a day from the sea.

After finding a place to park, Sara and Billy trudged up to the hill's bare spot to wait for Cathy. It didn't take long before Billy's grandfather, Scotty, spotted them. Seeing Sara and Billy, he walked toward them and yelled out for all to hear within two hundred yards, "THERE'S MY GRANDSON BILLY JONES, THE WORLD'S BEST SLEDDER!"

Sara, out of embarrassment, turned her head to look around as if Scotty were talking to someone else.

"Hi, Billy, and you too, daughter-in-law. Where's the supposed head of the household?" he promptly asked with his usual scurrilous demeanor.

"Not feeling well," Sara answered as Billy drifted off to meet with his friend Ryan, standing a few feet away.

"Not feeling well?" Scotty refuted. "I'll bet he stayed home because he's afraid to embarrass himself out here with the real sledders. He was afraid to ride a sled when he was a kid."

Sara ignored Scotty's attitude from the first day she met him at the park's naming. She wrote him off as a pompous ass. She despised the day he became her father-in-law.

Looking over Scotty's shoulder, Sara eyed Cathy and Eric approaching.

"Hey guys," she yelled out as they approached.

"Hello, Scotty," Cathy said, sounding like a voice being forced to speak to her most hated acquaintance. Eric didn't say a word.

"So, what's your friend doing here with you," Scotty said, looking at Eric with a sneer.

"He's going sledding with Billy and me," Cathy answered, looking like daggers wanted to fly out of her eyes.

"Not with my grandson," Scotty said, standing in a defiant position. "He's not going anywhere with the likes of you. You can take your black ass and go sled somewhere else!"

Before Eric had time to even react, Arnold, from seemingly out of nowhere, stepped between the two.

"You may not like me," Arnold yelled at Scotty. "I can take that. But your grandson is only a few yards away listening to you talk like that. You're an embarrassment to everyone. Go home and stay away from my family and our friends. You're nothing but a racist bigot!"

Scotty glared at him, then looked around. Everyone within earshot had heard. Realizing he was outnumbered with both Eric and Arnold there, he bellowed out, "I was just joking around! Calm down." then walked off with a smile on his face.

Sara was speechless. She hugged Arnold, then looked him in the eyes. Words didn't need to be said.

"Come on. Let's go up to the top!" Arnold yelled to Billy, who rushed over, grabbing Arnold by the hand as they walked to the top of Brandywine Hill.

37

The sun shone brightly over the Carolinas this April day. In Torrid Hills, melted snow cascaded down the surrounding Blue Ridge, like mini waterfalls tricking over rocks and pebbles. Spring was in the air. Soon, Billy Jones would play "coach pitch" baseball. Soon, Arnold Jones would be his coach. Soon, Scotty Jones would be in the stands watching.

"Perhaps you might think about letting someone else coach Billy this season," Sara said quietly to Arnold, hoping he would agree.

"You can't be serious." Arnold shot back at Sara, feeling like he had been trampled over. "Why in hell's name would I let someone else coach Billy? You don't think I'm good enough?"

"No, it's not that," Sara said, trying to squirm her way out of what was becoming a contentious situation.

Feeling insulted by Sara's suggestion, Arnold shot back, "I guess you think I should let his grandfather coach him. Huh? If not, then what is it?"

"I'm just afraid that your father is going to intimidate you like he always has. And I know how it will upset you." Sara explained as she stood at the kitchen stove preparing dinner.

"I'll be ready for anything he wants to throw at me," Arnold said with agitation in his voice.

"Speaking of throwing, do you realize that you will have to throw the ball to the kids on your team when they are up at bat?" Sara explained to Arnold.

"And your point is?" Arnold said.

"I'm just saying that it will put a lot of pressure on you to throw strikes every time to the kids."

"I can do that. Hell, I've been throwing the ball to Billy out back with no problem."

"There's a big difference between throwing in the backyard and standing out on the field throwing to the kids at bat. People in the stands will be watching you like a hawk. And if you don't throw strikes, they'll come pouncing down on you like that hawk pounces on its prey. It can get ugly."

"You make me nervous just talking about it. But I'll be damned if I'm going to turn over the coaching to anyone." Arnold said to Sara. "I learned a lot in that coach's meeting this winter. I'll be doing the baseball coaches certification before the season starts. Hopefully, it will include a lot for coaches pitching to the kids."

"Well, good luck. You know I'll be praying for you." Sara said with a slight smirk on her face.

A week before the season started, all the Torrid Hills little "league coaches" had become certified by attending the new coaches program. Amazingly, no one complained.

"I liked the program." Renaldo Torres commented to Adrian Knox, his assistant coach. "It helped me understand how important it is, the way disputes are handled."

"Yeah," Adrian said. "I was surprised when the guy they had to speak to us said that we were no different than the classroom teachers. I liked it when he said that youth sports is an outdoor classroom. I guess he's right. We're teaching these kids about a lot of things."

"You went to school with Arnold Jones, right?" Renaldo asked Adrian.

"Yeah, why do you ask?

174

"Remember when he was playing baseball, and his dad would yell at him all the time?"

"Yeah, man, I felt terrible for Arnold. I mean, Scotty Jones might be considered a hero around town, but he sure was mean to Arnold. It taught me a lesson to never act like him around my kid. Honestly, I don't know how he took it."

As Billy finished his breakfast, Arnold yelled out, "Okay, let's get at it, Billy."

"Do we have to practice today, Dad?" Billy replied. "Tommy and me were going to go down to the creek over by Clemens Street and find rocks."

"Now, how are you going to get better at baseball by throwing rocks?" Arnold said, looking frustrated that Billy wasn't excited about the upcoming baseball season.

"Let's get one thing straight, Billy. We signed you up for baseball, so you are going to play. That's it. It's called commitment."

"But you signed me up, Dad," Billy said. "I didn't like it last time when people laughed at us kids because we couldn't hit the ball."

"It's gonna be different this time because I'm going to pitch the ball. All the coaches get to pitch the ball this time." Arnold replied.

"But you don't know how to pitch the ball. That's what Grandpa said at the park."

Billy's remark traveled through Arnold like he had been hit in the stomach by a line drive from a major league hitter.

"Grandpa said that you could never play any good, so he wanted to be my coach. Can he, Dad?"

With a fit of anger, Arnold jumped from his chair and grabbed Billy by both arms. Shaking him, he yelled, "Don't you ever say that again, or I'll slap your face until it's beet red. YOU HEAR ME?"

Sara rushed to the room as Billy, unable to catch his breath, suddenly turned pale and cold. He was in shock, never experiencing his father's violent anger before.

Arnold looked in terrifying silence as Sara comforted Billy. Soon Billy's color came back. He stared at Arnold with the look of someone who had seen a ghost.

"I'll play baseball, Dad." was all Billy could say as he walked to his room with tears rolling down his face.

Sara motioned for Arnold to come into the kitchen.

"Close the door, Arnold," she said with a voice that belied her deep anger.

Arnold sat staring at the wall. Visions of apples rolling from a tree flooded his mind again. *He was Scotty Jones.*

Sara, not wanting to escalate the situation, suggested that Arnold make an appointment to see Dr. Monroe.

"It's something you have to do, Arnold." She said calmly, not wanting things to get worse. "Billy needs you now more than ever."

Arnold numbed from the experience, rose from his chair, nodded to Sara as if to agree, then walked toward the bedroom. He wouldn't reappear until the following day. An apology to Billy would have to wait.

"This is Arnold Jones; would Dr. Monroe have time to meet with me today?"

After what seemed like hours, the assistant said, "Can you make it at 6PM? She has a full schedule today but says she will stay after hours to meet with you."

"I'll be there," Arnold replied, his voice sullen and cheerless.

Before leaving for work at the motel, Arnold waited until Billy came down for breakfast.

Feeling shame and unworthiness, Arnold struggled to say the words, "I'm sorry Billy for the way I behaved last night."

"That's okay, Dad," Billy responded. "Can I go to the creek with Tommy today?"

The request stunned Arnold. He thought how foolish it was for him to get upset at Billy for something he wanted to do. At the end of the day, Billy was only seven years old …just a kid. "Sure, you can, Billy," he replied.

38

"Dr. Monroe will see you now." her assistant announced to Arnold.

"Thank you for taking the extra time to meet with me, Dr. Monroe." A contrite Arnold announced.

"I suppose it's something serious." Dr. Monroe offered.

"Yes, it is," Arnold admitted. "Last night, I completely lost it. I grabbed my son and shook him because he said he might want my father to be his coach. I have gotten angry before, but never to this extent."

"Maybe coaching the team is something you should put off this year, Arnold. You should think about what's best for Billy." Dr. Monroe offered.

"You wouldn't be suggesting that I let my father be his coach instead of me, are you?" Arnold, sounding impatient, replied.

"Arnold, I could prescribe medication to calm you down when these situations occur. But I'm afraid it would be like putting a band-aid on a broken leg. The best way to prevent these episodes concerning your father is to drop the idea of you coaching your son. At least for this year. Your father has a grip on you, and it appears he is not about to loosen up."

"I'm not letting him coach my son. I'd rather die! I'll show you all, especially my father, that I am a good coach and a way better father than he was!"

He stormed out of the doctor's office without offering a goodbye or thank you and sped home.

"So, how did things go with Dr. Monroe?" Sara asked as Arnold walked in the door.

Arnold didn't want to leave a hint that, according to him, he and Dr. Monroe were finished. "Fine." He answered quickly, then continued, "I'm ready for the big opening on Saturday."

"So she thinks it's still a good idea for you to coach?" Sara asked skeptically.

"Yes, it's all good," Arnold replied again quickly. "I won't let anything like what happened with Billy ever occur again. I promise." He said, looking straight at Sara and meaning every word.

Sixty-four kids signed up for the Torrid Hills coach pitch program. The stands would be filled for the opening game on Saturday morning. Arnold could hardly contain himself. "C'mon, Billy. What do you say we go out in the backyard and practice our hitting and catching? Let's show everyone in Torrid Hills that you might be the next Babe Ruth."

Billy and Arnold stood in the backyard throwing ball after ball at each other for over an hour.

"Nice catch Billy," Arnold would yell as Billy's catching skills improved with every throw.

"Time to call it a day," Arnold yelled to Billy as he scooped up the last grounder Arnold threw at him.

"I'm glad you are coaching me, Dad; I didn't want Grandpa to be my coach."

"Looks like you're improving, Billy." Sara complimented Billy as they walked in the door. "I watched you out the back window. You never missed catching the ball!"

"Yeah, Dad is a good coach." He replied, causing a warm smile to spread across Arnold's face.

It couldn't have been a more beautiful day in Torrid Hills. Bluer than blue can be, and not a cloud was in sight. The sun's rays erased the last glistening drops of dew covering the Scotty Jones Park infield. It was opening day for baseball.

Along with Billy's grandma Amanda, Torrid Hills' most dedicated baseball parents began to fill the stands. The smell of french fries and hotdogs filled the air at the newly built concession stand. In it, cooking away, was Rita Longworth, who volunteered her services to the rec department.

"What a nice person she is," Cathy stated. "It takes people like Rita to make these programs a success."

Sara had directed Cathy to recruit officials for all baseball games. Not an easy task since being an official meant, sometimes, having to take abuse from coaches and parents. To make things fair, each parent was assigned a turn officiating. Today's turn was Billy's grandpa, Dr. Jeff. As the teams took to the field, Dr. Jeff, trying his best to create a major league ballpark atmosphere, bellowed out, "PLAY BALL."

Scotty Jones was seated in the stands, anxious to disrupt the positive vibes running throughout the crowd. Regaling in the adulations that his loyal followers showered on him, Scotty soon announced, "It will only be a matter of time before my son makes a fool of himself. I can't wait to see him try to throw a pitch across the plate. Those poor kids will have to stand there forever before they can take a swing at the ball."

Arnold's team, the Badgers, took the infield, and Rock Spinnet was the first to pitch for the opposing team, the Sharks. Rock had been an infielder for one of the Atlanta Braves farm teams for eleven grueling years. Riding from game to game in a beat-up bus while barely making enough money, he promised himself not to give up. Never wanting to give up his dream, he vowed to continue until he was called up to the big-league team in Atlanta. At thirty- three years old, he finally faced reality. He returned to Torrid Hills to work at his dad's automotive shop.

The crowd cheered as Rock took the mound to throw to the players on the Sharks. The appreciation they had for Rock's dedication to the game was heartwarming. Everyone had hoped that someday he would be their local star. But the star faded away as the fact that only two percent of players signing a contract ever made it to the major league level became a reality.

Rock had no trouble hitting the strike zone of the players on the Sharks, who were loaded with a lot of talented kids. Not to mention early maturers. Finally, after the score was 13-0, the Badgers came to bat. Amanda sat up and leaned forward when it was Billy's turn to hit. Nelson Gibbens was the first assigned to pitch for the Badgers. There were two outs, and Billy had a chance to keep his team on the field. That is if he got a hit. Expecting the worst-case scenario, Scotty sat rubbing his hands down his pant legs. The next sound heard was the ball bouncing off Billy's bat. The ball soared to the outfield as Billy rounded first base. The thunderous roar from the crowd could be heard down on Brandywine Hill as Billy rounded second, then third base heading for home. Crossing home plate, an excited Scotty Jones ran out of the stands, grabbed Billy, lifted him to the sky, and yelled, "THAT'S MY GRANDSON! I MADE HIM THIS GREAT BALLPLAYER!"

A scared Billy ran to the dugout while umpiring Dr. Jeff motioned for Scotty to get back in the stands.

It was all Arnold could do to contain himself. While Scotty walked toward the stands waving his ballcap to the crowd, like a bolt of lightning, Arnold rushed toward Scotty. When reaching him, he tackled him to the ground with the force of an NFL linebacker. The spectators stood in awe, like they had seen a tornado coming at them. Several coaches quickly pulled Arnold off as he screamed, "I HATE YOU!" at Scotty.

"Hey, maybe you should have tried football." Scotty chided Arnold, grinning ear to ear as he walked back to the stands.

Cathy called Sara immediately and urged her to come to the park. Meanwhile, Dr. Jeff talked to Arnold to make sure he was okay to keep going.

"I'm fine." Arnold insisted. "I'm really sorry I lost it."

"I don't think anyone blames you." Dr. Jeff observed.

The game proceeded with Arnold up next to do the pitching for the Badgers. Scotty returned to his seat, never conjuring the thought that he had been, at the very least, an embarrassment to the day's event. Hearing that Arnold would be the next pitcher, Scotty couldn't wait for the moment to pounce on him like a vulture on its next victim.

Bryan Tolliver stood at the plate for the Sharks as Arnold began his role as the pitcher. Unable to shake Scotty's episode from his mind, Arnold struggled to get the ball over the plate. Bryan stood waiting ball after ball as Scotty sat in the stands with his bellowing laugh aimed at each of Arnold's pitches. A frustrated Arnold looked over to Jim Reingold, "Sorry, Jim, I'm too shook up by my father's behavior. I hope you don't mind taking over my spot."

"Quitter" Scotty yelled for all to hear as Arnold walked off the mound. At that, Melinda Summers, who had been sitting in the stands four rows behind Scotty, walked toward him and whispered something in his ear. Without hesitation, Scotty got up and walked from the stands to his car, and drove off.

"Did I just see that happen?" a bowled-over Alice Tolliver whispered to her sister Nancy, next to her. "What could Melinda possibly have said to him?" The rest of the crowd sat in wonder as the town's hero suddenly seemed to have lost his luster.

Game score at the finish? Badgers 18. The Sharks 13.

Walking from the stands to their cars, it appeared folks were returning from a funeral. The gossipy murmur would certainly not be about today's game. Scotty Jones won in that contest.

When Sara reached the park, she rushed to Arnold, who sat frozen with his head in his hands. "Are you okay?" she asked him.

Looking directly into Sara's eyes, he said, "I'm never okay as long as that man's alive."

"Why did you tackle Grandpa?" Billy asked as he ran over to see Sara and Arnold.

"I'm sorry, Billy. I shouldn't have done that, but I lost my temper. It upset me when Grandpa grabbed you." Arnold explained, hating that Billy had seen him like that. "Why don't you run over and play with your teammates while we stay and talk for a minute."

Not wanting to interfere, Amanda and Jeff walked slowly to their car, heads shaking with every step.

After thanking the volunteers for the day, Cathy walked over to Sara and Arnold and, in typical Cathy fashion, said, "What the hell do you think that woman said to Scotty?"

"What woman?" Sara asked.

"Over there in the blue dress. Melinda, something." Cathy replied. "She whispered something to Scotty that scared him off. What do you think it was?"

"I don't know, but I'm sure going to find out," Sara answered. "You remember, right?"

Looking befuddled, Cathy said, "Remember what?"

"Remember when we had the coaches' meeting, and Scotty gave us a hard time? Well, she's the woman who came over to us and said how proud she was that we stood up to Scotty and said if I ever have any problem with him, just give her a call." Sara replied, giving Arnold a hopeful look.

"Let's go home, Billy," Sara yelled. "Mommy has to get back to her office."

She held Arnold's hand as the three walked the usual path home.

Billy trotted ahead, and as they neared home, the sky suddenly darkened. Perhaps an omen as to what was to come.

39

Sara couldn't wait to get to her office. Running the whole way from home, "Hey Emma, Sara here." she said rapidly, breathing into her cell phone like she had just completed a hundred-yard dash. "Remember the story you told me about Melinda Summers?"

"Why do you ask?" replied Emma.

"Scotty Jones caused a disruption this morning at the game. Arnold tackled him after Scotty grabbed Billy and scared him. I wasn't there, but it was apparently a mess. Coaches had to pull Arnold off of Scotty. Cathy said Melinda was sitting in the stands, unbeknownst to Scotty, I'm sure. She walked over to Scotty when he started harassing Arnold again and whispered something in his ear. Cathy said he abruptly left the park after that."

"Oh, now this is going to be interesting. Then what happened?" Emma asked.

"Nothing."

"Nothing?" Emma, impatient as a butterfly, retorted. "Then why are you telling me all this?"

"Because I need to find out what Melinda whispered to Scotty," Sara replied. "If you talk to Melinda or hear anything, will you please let me know?"

"Look, if there is anything I can find out that might help get Scotty to stop abusing the hell out of Arnold, I'm all in." Emma answered.

"Thanks, Emma. I'm just afraid Arnold's getting to a breaking point."

Curiosity getting the best of her, Sara picked up the phone first thing Monday and called Melinda Summers.

"Hi, this is Melinda," the voice on the other end said. "How can I help you?"

"Good morning, Melinda," Sara replied. "This is Sara Tobin at the rec department."

Sara sat back with a look of surprise on her face when Melinda said. "Hi Sara, I was expecting your call. I'm assuming you're calling about the incident at the park Saturday."

"As a matter of fact, I am," Sara said. "I was hoping that if you had the time, we might meet to discuss the incident. It is both from the rec department perspective and a personal one."

"You name the time and place, and I'll be there." Melinda stated. "You do remember the promise I made that if Scotty Jones ever gave you trouble, I'd be there to help you?"

"Yes, I sure do, and I'm looking forward to meeting with you to discuss. How about my office tomorrow morning at nine?" Sara, anxiously awaiting an affirmative reply, said to Melinda.

"See you at nine." Melinda agreed.

Still upset from the disappointing event with Arnold and Scotty Saturday morning, Sara decided to stop by to see her mother.

"Hey, Mom. I thought I'd take a chance to see if you were free. I wanted your advice."

"You caught me at a good time. So, what's up?" replied Amanda.

"You were there Saturday morning, so I know you saw Arnold tackle Scotty. The season is only beginning, and I am very concerned that things will get worse."

"Yeah, we all saw it. Your father-in-law is a sick man. I mean to bully his own son the way he does is criminal. And I do mean criminal.

There is something deep-rooted in that man, causing him to behave the way he does. And he'll continue until Arnold retaliates far more than the way he did on Saturday."

"I'm at a loss," Sara responded. "But my biggest fear is Arnold will end up being the same way toward Billy?"

"Sometimes seeing the results of someone's awful behavior can help a person overcome that behavior, vowing to never be like that. Knowing Arnold, I think he is on that path." Amanda suggested. "I'm sure you'll be a big help to him in the process."

"We talk a lot about it," Sara replied. "Arnold tries so hard to be a good dad and not repeat anything that Scotty did to him. But he struggles."

Sara left feeling a little better. She vowed to help Arnold never duplicate his father's abusive behavior.

"Wow, you're taking off early this morning. You're meeting with Melinda first thing?" Arnold remarked to Sara.

"Yep, I'll tell you about it when I get home tonight. You'll make sure Billy gets to school on time, right?"

Sara, as with every morning, walked to work. This morning she was a half hour early. The cool breeze blowing down from the mountains made her feel invigorated. Feeling confident that Melinda may have a solution to the Scotty problem made the walk even more stimulating. Once reaching the office, she said her usual hello to the receptionist, who quickly replied, "You have a visitor in your office." Alarmed and embarrassed, she entered her office saying, "So sorry I'm late." She was taken aback when noticing it wasn't Melinda. "I'm sorry, who are you?" She asked with a fluttery feeling in her stomach.

"I'm an attorney representing Scotty Jones. He has advised that I tell you he will be suing your husband for attacking him and causing bodily harm. Also, he will be suing the rec department as they are liable for allowing the incident Saturday to occur on rec department property."

"Leave this office immediately, ma'am," Sara said, as rage whistled through her like wind on a nighttime desert.

It was interesting to see the attorney and Melinda pass each other as they entered and exited Sara's office.

"Please have a seat," Sara pleaded with Melinda as she entered her office. "I need a minute to calm down."

"If you don't mind my asking, who was that I just passed?" Melinda requested.

"Scotty Jones's attorney," Sara replied as if she were referring to someone who might be her worst enemy.

"Interesting," Melinda replied. "Let me get right to the point, Sara. I have witnessed Scotty Jones's behavior long before I became a member of the city council. It doesn't surprise me that he has sent someone here to threaten you. It's unfortunate that he happens to be your father-in-law. However, after Saturday's fiasco, I am going to present evidence that Scotty should be arrested for a crime he committed. That crime was a hit and run, and it involved me." Melinda continued. "I recently received some evidence from a friend at the police department. They looked at the video surveillance from the intersection on that night, and it clearly shows Scotty chasing me down the street, then ramming into the back of my car, causing me to hit a tree, then fleeing the scene."

Sara sat stunned. She had heard this story from Emma, but hearing there was evidence changed everything. She finally responded, "Yes, he is my father-in-law. But he has wreaked havoc on our family for years by tormenting my husband, as you witnessed Saturday. Nothing would please us more than to see him pay the price for his behavior."

"Don't worry about any legal action he has proposed against Arnold or your department. I will be meeting with him this morning to warn him of the consequences of threatening you. Once I have his signed agreement, I will surprise him with my own suit of causing me bodily harm and fleeing the scene."

"Oh my gosh, you are dead serious," Sara responded. "I didn't think anyone else would ever stand up to Scotty."

"It has to be done," Melinda said. "He has lived on his hero worship for too long."

As Melinda walked out the door, Sara thanked her for all her efforts.

"One last thing," Melinda said as she got outside. "Don't mention this conversation to anyone until we see Scotty Jones in prison."

"You have my word. Thank you again for all your effort." Sara said as Melinda walked to her car.

40

"All rise." The judge ordered. "Will the jury please present its findings?"

"Your honor, we, the jury, find the defendant Scotty Jones guilty on all charges of leaving the scene of an accident that resulted in serious bodily injury. The jurors recommend a full sentence of five years in prison."

The room broke out into turmoil, causing the judge to call for order in the court. Some in the crowd were weeping, while others cheered. Feeling vindicated by Scotty going to prison, Melinda glared at him with a taunting look, covering her mouth with her hands to hide the pleasureful smile behind them. With that, Scotty lost control. He jumped out of the witness stand and ran towards Melinda and Sarah, seated beside each other. With his fist clenched, he went to attack Melinda, but he was tackled and knocked to the ground by the court officer. The bailiff put Scotty in handcuffs and led him away.

Arnold stood shaking and began to turn white. "Arnold, are you okay?" Sara asked, worried by his stunned expression. He was still shocked at the trial's outcome and the sight of Scotty running toward Melinda and Sara with such hate in his eyes. He stood motionless, hoping to feel relief from the moment. It didn't come. As they led Scotty away, he found himself staring at the remorseless eyes of a defeated, sorrowful figure of the man he so often wanted to please. The beatings, humiliations, and never-ending lack of love from his past consumed him.

On the drive home, Arnold reflected on the events of the day. He felt relieved that Scotty wouldn't be around to bother him for the next five years. With Scotty gone, he no longer felt pressure to push Billy in sports. With that, Billy began to develop into a standout athlete, while Arnold focused on becoming a better father.

The summer after the trial, Arnold, Sara, and Billy decided to go to Belmont Park for a picnic. They invited their freshly engaged friends, Cathy, and Eric, to join them. After a fun day in the sunshine, the group parted ways. On the way home, Arnold suggested they ride by Walnut Street, where Torrid Hills's largest apple tree sat majestically in bloom at the top of a hill. Beneath the tree, Arnold, looking out the window, noticed several apples rotting away in the hot sun. Just as he turned away, an apple dropped and rolled down the hill far from the rest. Perhaps a metaphor for Arnold and his new life ahead.

Arnold Jones was named Coach of the Year by the Torrid Hills Little League, while Sara was promoted to Supervisor of Parks and Recreation when Emma moved with her partner to Omaha, Nebraska.

Billy Jones starred on his high school baseball team and earned a scholarship to the University Of North Carolina.

Cathy and Eric married, and Cathy moved to Platsburg, where she accepted the position of Recreation Director, with a raving review from Sara. Eric went on to run a campaign and was elected mayor of Platsburg.

Dr. Jeff and Amanda continued their successful practices in helping the people of Torrid Hills.

While in prison, Scotty Jones was found guilty of other charges and given a longer sentence. He wouldn't get to finish the sentence, as he died of a heart attack one year to the day after his initial incarceration.

ACKNOWLEDGEMENT

While she wouldn't let me put her name on the cover, my daughter Joanna was an amazing help in putting this book together. "Contributing Editor" just doesn't describe the numerous times I interrupted her at work, home and who knows where else to try to get things right. And I would be remiss if I didn't give thanks also to her daughter Jamie, who I predict will someday become an author, herself.

ABOUT THE AUTHOR

Fred Engh founded the National Alliance for Youth Sports (NAYS), America's leading advocate, since 1981, for positive and safe sports for youth in organized sports.

He initially created the National Youth Sports Coaches Association (NYSCA) in 1981 to help provide volunteer coaches with needed information on coaching children.

The organization evolved into the National Alliance for Youth Sports (NAYS) in 1993. Its innovative training programs for parents, administrators, and officials have been embraced and utilized in over 3,000 cities nationwide and on U.S. military bases worldwide.

In 1999 he authored *Why Johnny Hates Sports*, a first-of-its-kind look at the severe problems plaguing organized sports and, more importantly, how to correct them. In 2015 he wrote Unsinkable Spirit, which chronicles his incredible life story.

Through the years, he spoke at numerous national and international conferences, including the International Forum on Sport in Doha, Qatar, and the Pre-Olympic Symposium in Greece. He also frequently appeared on national television programs such as Good Morning America, CNN, ESPN's Outside the Lines, The Today Show, and ABC World News Tonight.

He has received many prestigious awards and honors throughout his career, including being named one of America's Top 100 sports educators, being chosen for the Youth Sports Hall of Fame, and being inducted into the University of Maryland Eastern Shore Sports Hall of Fame,

An accomplished athlete, he was a national prep school wrestling All-American at Mercersburg Academy. He also coached high school football, served as an athletic director, and held high-level positions with the Athletic Institute before creating NAYS,

He grew up in Ocean City, Maryland, and resides in West Palm Beach, Florida, with his wife, Michaele.

OTHER BOOKS BY FRED ENGH

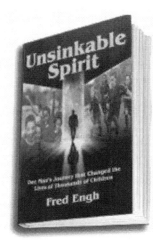

"Very seldom do you find someone who sees something wrong, then works diligently to make an impact in the right direction. It is inspiring and gives hope all in one quick read of a book. A personal story that hopefully will inspire many more people to follow their dreams" **G.G. Miami Fl.**

Mom's Choice Award

"This small book is suitable for adults and children. The author describes his 1961 enrollment in an all-black college on Maryland's Eastern Shore and his subsequent participation as the first white person to play on one of the college's athletic teams.".
Terry Parker

"The author has captured the raw feeling of life during the tumultuous years of WWII. From his childhood experiences, stories about young men and women shipped to the jungle warfare of the South Pacific, while leaving their loved ones at home pulls at ones heartstrings. Those who served, return home to a very different world".
Amazon reader

"Great book! It gives you an inside look, sometimes a comedic look, at why children seem to be losing interest in sports." **KB Albany Ga.**

"I really liked this book. Good stories, mystery, suspense, and insight into human nature -- you get all of this in this book that is unlike any other. It gives us thought-provoking insights wrapped in fast-paced entertainment -- and we sense that profound things are at play. Once you start reading, you can't put it down, as you get to know the "5 in the Corner".
Gerry Sullivan

"This book is perfect for my kindergarten classroom lessons about making new friends and also teaching the roles of author and illustrator! **LE Ocean City Md.**

"This is a brilliant book for anyone wondering about their own children's or the general experiences of children in sport,"
Bryan H. UK

"Every adult who has anything to do with coaching sports should be made to read this book."
Cindy C. US

"This is a book of resilience, determination, teamwork, friendship in all colors, and the ability to overcome racism. You will be hooked, like me, from the first page. I have read a couple of other books by this author and have enjoyed reading them as well."
Ek Greenville Tn.

"I follow Fred Engh as well as Todd van Linda's work. What a treat to have them both in one book! The refreshing wit of Engh combined with the sheer genius of van Linda's illustration makes for a wonderful read. This book will make a great gift for anyone on your list so I'm pre-ordering mine today".
JL Houston Tx

Made in the USA
Columbia, SC
07 June 2023

4f478e6c-302c-46f8-a166-b9783e59c4e9R02